"Open ▓▓▓▓▓▓
"I'm quite capable of—

Laughing softly, he took advantage of her open lips and fed her a mouthful of pancake from the plate he'd prepared.

Swallowing the delicious morsel, she gestured toward the tray. "What did I do to deserve such special treatment?"

"Because you're crazy and kind and work other people's shifts at the hospital. Or maybe I'm the one who's crazy." He hesitated for a moment. "Crazy about you."

Her senses skyrocketed, robbing her of a reply, so she silently allowed him to feed her. When she trusted herself to speak, she said, "You're a good cook," and reached for the fork, but he held it beyond her grasp.

"Did I mention this is breakfast for two? You have to share," he said.

She smiled, took the fork from his hand, and speared a generous helping. Holding one hand underneath to catch drips, she offered it to him. He closed his hand over hers, guiding the fork to his mouth.

She was mesmerized by the slow, sensual way he took the food between his lips. A flame began to burn in the pit of her stomach. Drew reached for her other hand, and her eyes widened with pleasurable shock as he nibbled a drop of syrup from her palm. . . .

WHAT ARE *LOVESWEPT* ROMANCES?

They are stories of true romance and touching emotion. We believe those two very important ingredients are constants in our highly sensual and very believable stories in the *LOVESWEPT* line. Our goal is to give you, the reader, stories of consistently high quality that may sometimes make you laugh, sometimes make you cry, but are always fresh and creative and contain many delightful surprises within their pages.

Most romance fans read an enormous number of books. Those they truly love, they keep. Others may be traded with friends and soon forgotten. We hope that each *LOVESWEPT* romance will be a treasure—a "keeper." We will always try to publish

LOVE STORIES YOU'LL NEVER FORGET
BY AUTHORS YOU'LL ALWAYS REMEMBER

The Editors

Loveswept ® 515

Theresa Gladden
Just Desserts

BANTAM BOOKS
NEW YORK · TORONTO · LONDON · SYDNEY · AUCKLAND

JUST DESSERTS

A Bantam Book / December 1991

If you would be interested in receiving protective vinyl
covers for your Loveswept books, please write to this address
for information:

Loveswept
Bantam Books
P.O. Box 985
Hicksville, NY 11802

ISBN 0-553-44176-0

Published simultaneously in the United States and Canada

Bantam Books are published by Bantam Books, a division of
Bantam Doubleday Dell Publishing Group, Inc. Its trademark,
consisting of the words "Bantam Books" and the portrayal of a
rooster, is Registered in U.S. Patent and Trademark Office and
in other countries. Marca Registrada. Bantam Books, 666
Fifth Avenue, New York, New York 10103.

PRINTED IN THE UNITED STATES OF AMERICA

OPM   0 9 8 7 6 5 4 3 2 1

For Dot and Leon Phillips

Many thanks to Carolyn Patrick and Debbie Williams, special friends who shared the New Orleans years with me and who first encouraged me to tell this story; and to Lisa Cantrell for her unwavering faith in my ability to write it.

One

He'd gone too far. She had no choice but to retaliate.

Caitlin MacKenzie sat on the floor, hidden behind the camelback sofa. Dressed cat burglar style in black from neck to toe, she felt slightly foolish and very much on edge. She'd never done this sort of thing before, and she just wanted to do it and get it over with.

Her gaze darted to the two items lying beside her. They looked harmless, appealing. The perfect weapons for a sweet revenge.

Revenge. Now that was an ugly word, Caitlin thought. Her arms tightened around her raised knees. She wasn't normally a vengeful person, but she had her limits and he'd gone beyond them. She couldn't allow him to continue his game of driving her mad. The only thing she could think of to stop him was payback in kind.

She hoped he arrived soon, before New Orleans's tropical humidity melted her resolve along with the rest of her. She slid her hand beneath her heavy chestnut hair, lifting it momentarily to catch the rush of air coming in through the open window in front of her.

October in New Orleans, she grumbled silently, was hotter than her north Georgia hometown in July. She thought longingly of the air conditioner, but she'd turned it off earlier and raised every window in the house. She grinned. She knew she'd done that just as much to annoy him as to save money.

The smile was replaced by a frown as her gaze returned to her weapons. So far, they appeared to be unaffected by the heat. She shook her head in exasperation. Of course, they were fine. She'd prepared them carefully, remembering to take the room's temperature into consideration. Conjuring up imaginary trouble was a nasty habit she needed to break.

Suddenly, she tensed at the sound of a finely tuned engine. Glancing out the window, she saw a silver Mercedes pull into the narrow driveway. The car quickly passed from her view around the side of the Victorian shotgun house.

Caitlin's heart jumped up into her throat. Adrenaline pumped through her veins.

Outside a car door slammed.

An attack of panic paralyzed her. Her courage wavered.

Stay cool, she counseled herself. Remember what he's done to you. She silently ticked off every torture she'd endured since she'd rented a room in his house a month ago, when her apartment building went condo. By the time she got to his latest despicable trick, she was ready to murder the bum. He deserved no mercy.

Her courage clicked firmly into place. Caitlin rose up onto her knees, poised to strike.

Heart beating a rapid tattoo, she listened to the front door creak open. Light flooded the foyer, sending fluorescent ribbons across the floor to her hiding place. She prayed he wouldn't alter his nightly ritual.

The steady tap of expensive shoes on wood echoed loudly in the stillness. She heard him enter the room. A bubble of nervous laughter formed in her throat, and she forced it down.

The sound of his footsteps ceased. Caitlin risked a peek around the edge of the sofa.

He was a dark silhouette standing beside an armchair and table near the fireplace. His white lab jacket stretched across his broad shoulders as he bent down to turn on a Capiz shell accent lamp.

Caitlin studied him in the dim glow of lamplight. His hair was the color of warm brandy, though a few streaks of premature silver winged back from his temples. It was cut with expert precision and styled to careless windblown perfection. Although she couldn't see his face, it was etched into her mind. His features were aristocratic, saved from appearing arrogant by a stamp of humor and an erotic mouth that laughed more often than it frowned.

He was nearly six feet tall. She disliked men who towered above her own five feet two inches. In her experience, tall men tended to view her as a cute little thing, someone to be picked up in a bear hug or patronized. But even with his height, she had to admit he was an attractive package of masculine flesh and bones. He certainly didn't look like a trickster devil.

He turned in her direction. Thinking she'd been spotted, she froze, her breath caught in her lungs. She shivered a little as she watched him glance around the room. She knew only too well his deceptively sleepy green eyes were quite capable of taking in more than what could be seen on the surface.

His gaze swept past the sofa, and she slowly let out her breath. Her relief was short-lived as the open window behind her caught his attention. Caitlin felt faint. If he made a move to shut it, she was dead.

He merely shook his head and began loosening his tie.

She relaxed her taut muscles. Perhaps luck was on her side tonight.

Sliding a hand beneath his lab jacket, he reached into his trouser pocket and withdrew a slim black wallet. He casually tossed it onto the table. Crumbled bills and a handful of change followed.

Caitlin leaned forward. Even though the man was driving her crazy, his nightly ritual fascinated her.

He delved into the lab jacket and produced a toy elephant. It was a shocking shade of pink. He settled it on the chair, giving its fuzzy rump a fond pat.

Raids on other pockets revealed sugarless gum, a kazoo, two plastic spiders, an ink pen in the shape of a hypodermic, Disney stickers, trick handcuffs, and a pair of fake glasses with a rubber nose and mustache attached.

As the items on the table piled higher, Caitlin spared a thought to the frantic hustle that would occur in the morning when he tried to repocket all his bizarre possessions.

"Damn," he said in his polite prep-school voice that barely hinted at his Southern heritage. "It's hotter than hell in here." His tone betrayed mild annoyance.

Good, she thought. Roast, you buzzard.

One last item emerged from his lab coat, a red crayon. He stripped off the coat and pitched it toward the chair, then aimed the crayon at the table.

The crayon missed its target and fell to the floor. He dropped to his knees to find it.

Caitlin scooped up one of her weapons and quietly eased from behind the sofa. She tiptoed within an arm's length and tapped him on the shoulder.

Captured crayon in hand, Drew Daniels looked up. "What do—" was all he had time to sputter before a pie smashed into his face.

Drew flinched at the impact, then went as still as if he'd been freeze-dried. For a second, his mind shut down in complete disbelief.

He heard the sound of something metallic hit the floor. His brain reactivated, and he slid his tongue along his lower lip. Bavarian cream pie. A gurgling noise, something between a laugh and a choke, rumbled in his throat.

"Gotcha!" he heard Caitlin exclaim, and recognized triumph laced with humor in her voice.

Well, I'll be damned, he thought. He'd spent the last four weeks trying to chip through his new housemate's steel-plated reserve and had almost given up hope of discovering her sense of humor. A ridiculous surge of pleasure raced along his veins. He stood up, feeling like a miner who'd just found the mother lode.

Raking pie from his face with one hand, he blinked his eyes open. The stuff clung to his lashes. He glanced around the room, searching for her. She was standing behind the sofa, arms hugged to her chest in an unconscious protective gesture.

As his gaze locked with hers, she inhaled sharply and stepped back until she encountered the wall. Her hands reached out to grasp the back of the sofa in a death grip. Drew wondered if she was contemplating throwing the furniture at him next.

"Congratulations." He smiled in admiration. "Few people have ever been able to catch me off guard long enough to belt me with a pie. I can't believe you did it."

Tension visibly left her body. She flashed a brief, saucy grin. "Want an instant replay?"

"I don't think so," he said, taking a few steps toward her. "That would be overkill. Never strike twice with the same gag. Keeps the victim off balance wondering what's going to happen next." He smiled, then continued, "Take you, for example. Right now, you're busy worrying about what I'm going to do to settle the score."

Caitlin's gaze flickered over his face. He was teasing her again, she decided. She glanced at his right hand. "What are you going to do? Color me to death?"

He looked down at the red crayon in his hand, then back to her with a grin. "Maybe later. Might be fun. A little kinky, but fun." He put the crayon in his pants pocket.

She laughed, and Drew was enchanted by the crystal sound. Her somber view of the world didn't allow her to laugh easily. Even her hazel eyes, which usually held an enigmatic expression, were bright with amusement.

He inched another step closer. "I suggest we declare a truce. Negotiate a peaceful settlement."

"In your dreams, Daniels," she shot back.

"My, my. Such sarcasm from the earnest Dr. MacKenzie." Drew ran a practiced eye over her. She had a softly rounded face with the kind of skin and bone structure that aged gracefully. Her small frame was delicately formed but deliciously curved in all the right places. Her eyes intrigued him most, though. They changed color at whim. Right now they were doe brown and amber with the merest hint of green. Red-gold highlights kept her long, wavy hair from being plain brown. Though she usually wore her hair in a prissy French braid, tonight it tumbled seductively down her back.

He watched her stubborn chin lift at his scrutiny. His admiration for her grew. A lot of determination and tenacity was packed inside her small body.

He grinned. "Come on. There's no reason to hide behind the sofa all night."

Caitlin fought the urge to respond to that persuasive grin with one of her own. "I don't trust you. I'm staying right here."

"Now, Catie—"

"Don't call me Catie!"

Her outburst made him laugh. He knew he shouldn't tease her so unmercifully, but it was the only way to get a reaction out of her.

"I've told you," she said, lifting her head to a regal height, "no one calls me Catie."

"I do." He leisurely crossed the remaining foot between him and the sofa.

She ducked down, disappearing from sight.

Drew chuckled. His amusement quickly faded, though, as she popped up with another pie in her hand. He made a rapid jerking motion to the right, then reached over the sofa, anticipating a counter-move from her.

She barely evaded him. "Back off, buster. Another tacky trick like that, and you'll wear more humble pie."

"What'd I ever do to you?" he asked, holding out his arms.

Caitlin stared at him incredulously. The man was a menace! His lazy green eyes and come-hither smile ought to be gracing a wanted poster in the post office. "I can forgive most of your juvenile stunts," she said, "but running my name through a computer dating service was despicable."

"Are you still mad about that?" He looked as if he couldn't possibly imagine her remembering such a trivial event. "That was ages ago."

"Last week," she corrected him. "I'm not mad. I'm getting even. You're getting your just desserts."

Drew grinned. A practical joke and a pun all in the same night. She was finally loosening up. "Holding a grudge can give you ulcers. Trust me." He patted the stethoscope draped around his neck. "I'm a doctor. I know these things."

"You're a pediatrician," she said dryly. "I doubt your patients get ulcers."

He shook his head. "It's a weird world. Even kids get stressed out these days."

"They probably see you coming and get stressed out."

"Not nice," he chided, wagging a finger at her. "My patients love me."

She rolled her eyes. "Every kid loves a circus, I guess."

"Are you calling me a clown?" Maybe he did try to clown his way through life, but he didn't like the idea of her trying to pigeonhole him that way.

"If the floppy shoes fit . . ."

His brows rose. "At least I have a sense of humor."

The implication that she didn't stabbed at her, then fell away. This revenge thing simply wasn't going the way she'd imagined. He was supposed to be apologizing, not acting like it was a great lark.

They stared at each other. Minutes crept by.

Caitlin didn't know what to do. Drew seemed completely relaxed. A slight smile crinkled the corners of his mouth. He was getting a kick out of the whole thing, she realized. If the circumstances were reversed, she would be enraged. Perhaps, Drew Daniels had something she lacked—an innate ability to appreciate the absurdity in a situation and laugh at himself.

She shifted nervously from one foot to the other, suddenly extremely conscious of Drew and her unnatural role as prankster.

He raised his eyebrows in a manner that said it was time to ante up or fold. "Well?"

She sighed. "Oh, all right. Promise you'll stop

playing tricks on me. No more bathrooms filled with inflatable beach balls. No more computer dates."

"I am sorry about that. The computer date business did get a little out of hand." He flashed her a wide grin. "I didn't mean any harm. I just thought you needed a little more fun in your life. You're always so serious." He made serious sound like a social disease.

She merely looked at him coldly.

"I had your best interests at heart," he went on. "Okay, I admit the guy the dating service sent didn't work out. Maybe I filled out the forms wrong." Of course he had. Finding her the perfect date hadn't been his objective. If she saw a good example of a turkey, maybe he'd begin to look good to her.

"That man was bizarre," Caitlin said. Her arm ached from holding the pie aloft, and she lowered it to rest on top of the sofa.

He laughed, showing an orthodontist's nightmare of perfectly even teeth. "Okay, you're right. He was a little different, even for an artist."

Her eyes narrowed, and she strode out from behind the sofa. "'A little different' doesn't begin to describe that creature."

"What didn't you like?" he asked. "His Mardi-Gras purple, green, and gold hair? He was a happening dude." She grimaced with distaste. "I thought it was very nice of him to offer to paint you in the nude," Drew added. "Though why he wanted to be nude when he painted you, I can't imagine."

She groaned. "Give me a break, Daniels."

He laughed and took a step toward her. "I really am sorry. It was a rotten thing to do. Forgive me?"

Her gaze locked with his. His soft plea and coaxing smile seemed genuine. Any leftover resentment she harbored melted. "All right. I forgive you."

"Even-steven?" He extended his hand to shake on their truce.

Caitlin put her free hand in his. Immediately, she recognized it was a grave tactical error as he quickly snatched the pie out of her other hand.

She jerked away. Heart in her throat, she backed up. He'd done it to her again! Conned her right into his web with his sexy smile and fast-talking.

Drew advanced, testing the weight of the pie. A mischievous grin plastered itself to his deceiving face.

Caitlin shook her head. Her hands came up as if to ward off an attack. "Now, Drew, you're the one who called a truce. You said we were even-steven."

"I lied." His eyebrows wiggled, and he flicked imaginary ashes from an imaginary cigar à la Groucho Marx.

She darted behind a paisley print Queen Anne chair. "You really don't want to hit me with that pie, do you?"

"Yes, I do." He nodded solemnly, then stepped up on the chair cushion, scaring an involuntary shriek out of her. "No need to scream, my dear," he said, lapsing into a dreadful German accent. "It vill do no good. Ve're all alone, *Liebchen.* Come-in-zee here and you vill get un nice pie."

Caitlin inched backward toward the entrance way and bumped into the doorframe. In an astonishing move that made her feel as if her eyes would pop out, he tipped the chair over onto its back and hopped down. She edged out into the foyer, turned, and ran.

Shouting, "Tallyho," Drew took off after her.

The hallway seemed endless. Her pulse beat triple time. She heard him closing in on her, laughing and calling her name.

She desperately eyed her bedroom just beyond the

dining alcove. As she sped toward it, she almost tripped over an Oriental carpet runner.

Drew caught up with her, grabbing a fistful of her shirt.

She staggered backward, bumping into him. When she tried to pull away, she lost her balance and fell to the floor.

He went down with her, still holding on to her shirt. Throwing one leg over her thighs, he blocked her attempt to rise. She tried to knock the pie out of his hand, but he held it over his head beyond her reach.

In silent desperation, she turned her face to the large hand now gripping her shoulder and sank her teeth into his wrist.

"Ouch!" he yelped. "No fair biting."

"Then let go," she said, struggling uselessly against his greater strength.

"I'll let go if you say uncle."

"Never." The muscles in her arms ached from the strain of pushing against his shoulders.

He laughed, fueling her determination not to give in. Using her last bit of energy, she tried to shove him off balance. Her rapid movement dislodged the pie.

They both grabbed for it at the same time. They both missed. The pan flipped over and descended.

"No!" she screamed just before it landed on her face.

Shock radiated through her body. Cloying sweet cream filled her nose and open mouth. She gagged, then swallowed spasmodically.

"Oh my God," she heard him mumble. Then she felt him trembling. The wretch was laughing! she thought. She'd strangle him as soon as she was able to breathe.

The pie pan slid down the front of her shirt until it was trapped between their bodies. Blindly she reached for it. Her hand came in contact with his stomach, and she gasped.

His fingers closed over hers. He took the pan out of her hand and tossed it aside.

Gaining some semblance of control, Caitlin wiped cream from her eyes. Opening them carefully, she saw Drew's face contorted with an effort not to laugh.

With more outward calm than she felt, she casually reached for the tie hanging around his neck and used it to mop up more pie.

Drew's lips twitched, then a deep resonant laugh rumbled out.

She began laughing, too, and inhaled cream pie. A burning sensation spread through her lungs. She choked and coughed.

"Catie," he said, wrapping his arms around her, supporting her. "Are you all right?"

Instinctively, she leaned against him, clinging to the comfort he offered. Her coughing fit subsided. She could breathe again.

Drew hugged her tight, gently rubbing her back. His concern for her did not entirely blot out his awareness of how good it felt to hold her. Her wild cloud of hair shimmered in his vision.

Caitlin suddenly became conscious of being held. Her forehead rested intimately in the curve of his neck. Her arms encircled his shoulders. He felt warm and solid, and as she breathed in his scent, she detected the smell of soap and spice mixed with sweet cream. A physical reaction, swift, violent, and purely sensual, entered her bloodstream and rushed straight for her brain.

In a distant corner of her mind, she heard him whisper her name, felt his lips upon her hair. He lifted his hands to her shoulders, and she slowly looked up into his eyes.

Oh, no, she thought, recognizing that he, too, felt

the chemistry flowing between them. She glanced away, running fingers along her temple.

"Catie, look at me," he said softly.

She didn't respond. Awareness of the proximity of their bodies occupied her mind. Every fiber of her being was caught up in the pressure of his masculine leg straddling her thighs, his gentle hand curved around her neck, and the tingling sensation bringing her nerve endings to life.

For a second, she closed her eyes, trying to deny her conflicting emotions. Then she took a deep breath and looked at him.

Her gaze locked with his, and tension invaded her limbs. She could swear the air became heavier, more difficult to breathe.

Bemused, Drew watched the hint of green in her eyes begin to glow like a polished gem. It was emerald fire. It beckoned him, called his name. Impelled by the dynamic summons, he answered without hesitation and slowly lowered her to the floor.

Caitlin barely registered his weight pressing her spine to the hardwood boards. Her mind was too busy reacting to currents, closing doors on protests that skittered here and there, shutting off alarms, feeling so very much *alive.*

Resting his elbows on the floor, Drew cradled her face in his hands. He was entranced by the richness of her eyes, the ivory of her skin. "Catie." Her name was a whisper of breath against her lips.

"Hmmm?" Had she responded aloud? Caitlin wondered. She didn't know. Mesmerized by his inquisitive fingers stroking lightly along her cheekbones, she gave up trying to think clearly. Her gaze drifted to his mouth. An unusual solemnness hovered there.

He was going to kiss her, she thought. How nice. Her eyes closed with a will of their own.

The first touch of his mouth was a gentle experiment. Feather soft, yet warm, caressing. Her hands slid up his arms, kneaded his shoulders. The subtle intricacy of the kiss saturated her senses and invoked an incredible response she hadn't known she was capable of giving. Beneath the steady, inducing pressure of his mouth, her lips parted, accepting, taking, giving in return.

She felt his palm at the base of her throat, his thumb drifting lightly along the underside of her jaw. A murmur of protest escaped her as his mouth left hers.

Drew nibbled at the sweet creamy confection clinging to her cheek, then kissed a path to her eyelids. Her lashes fluttered upon his lips, soft as a whisper of butterfly wings. He threaded his fingers through her hair, reveling in its silkiness. Need curled inside him. Now he knew why she appealed to him so. She was honey and liquid fire. He covered her mouth with his again, and his sense of time splintered. He felt a sensation not unlike shooting stars or free-falling through space.

Caitlin began to tremble. She delighted in and yet feared a desire so vivid, it took tangible shape and beat in rhythm with her heart. For one irrefutable moment her spirit shed its shackles and complexities to fuse with his. It was too powerful for her to handle. The feeling hurled her back into reality.

Caitlin broke the contact and turned her head away, not wanting him to look at her with those eyes that saw so clearly beneath the surface. Feeling self-conscious, she let go of him, her arms drifting to her sides.

Drew stroked her face in a last caress, then reluctantly rolled away to lie beside her.

Eyes shut tight, she listened to his ragged breathing. Her own was none too steady. She willed her body to cease trembling, but discovered the body was in mutiny with the mind's command.

Abandoning her inner struggle, she allowed herself to acknowledge her reaction. Simple physical attraction was a pale description. She felt stunned. Distance, she thought. That was what she needed. Some time alone to think.

She slowly sat up, then stood. Without a word, she headed for her bedroom.

Drew called out to her as she disappeared into her room and closed the door. He drew in an unsteady breath and stared up at the swirling pattern on the ornate ceiling.

How badly had he screwed up this time? he wondered. He shouldn't have kissed her. But as he'd looked into her intriguing eyes, he'd acted on an impulse he'd been wanting to follow for weeks.

He ran one of his sticky hands through his hair. She had singed him with her fire, burning an indelible mark on his mind. He now had her attention. So how was he going to prevent her from retreating behind her reserved facade?

Two

"Kissed by a clown," Caitlin murmured. She combed her fingers through her freshly washed hair as she paced her room. A shower and an hour of thinking had done little to lessen her confusion over her reaction to kissing Drew. Heaven help her, but she'd loved every second of it.

She scooped up a brush from her vanity table, then sat down on the edge of the four-poster bed dominating the small room. A million questions bumped into one another in her mind. The answers she came up with were muddier than the Mississippi River.

Her fingers shook as she brushed tangles from her hair. She'd been able to wash away every trace of Bavarian cream pie, but banishing Drew from her thoughts wasn't so easy.

Caitlin thoughtfully tapped the brush against her palm. At twenty-nine, she was no stranger to the man-woman chemistry. An encounter like tonight's hadn't sent her into such an adolescent orbit in years.

Instinct told her to proceed cautiously. She simply

didn't indulge in casual affairs. Not just because of her upbringing, but also for the sake of her self-esteem. Nor would she allow biology to ruin a potential friendship. She also had to consider the fact that Drew was her landlord and they occupied the same house.

Relationships were hell on the nerves, she thought, and she had no idea how she wanted to handle this one.

A flat-handed slap on the door almost sent her flying off the bed. She tossed the brush onto the pointed-star quilt, then padded barefoot across the floor.

"What?" She sounded neither gracious nor welcoming.

"May I come in?" Drew's well-modulated voice was once again prep-school polite.

Her gaze flew to the oval mirror on her vanity table. She grimaced at what she saw. An oversized football jersey, worse the wear from numerous washings, covered her decently enough. But combined with her wet hair and bare feet, she felt at a distinct disadvantage. "No. What do you want?"

"Mind closing your window? The air conditioner is on."

"It's closed." She didn't have the energy to argue about high electric bills. "I heard it kick on earlier."

"Okay," he said. "Oh, and don't worry about cleaning up the pie mess. I took care of it."

"You did?" She was amazed. He was more of the let-it-lie-where-it-falls type.

"Uh-huh. Are you hungry?"

She couldn't imagine sitting calmly across the dinner table from him tonight. "No. No, I'm not."

"Suit yourself."

She breathed a sigh of relief as she heard him walk away. Her relief was cut short by his immediate return and another one of his flat-handed knocks.

"Catie, your car isn't parked outside. Are you having trouble with it again or did you leave it somewhere?"

She leaned her forehead against the door. How could she have forgotten about it? "I parked it on Napoleon Street this afternoon so you would think I wasn't home."

He laughed, murmured something she didn't catch, then said, "Give me your keys. I'll jog over and drive it home."

"No," she shouted back. "I'll go." She raced to the closet and grabbed a pair of well-worn jeans.

"Don't be crazy." Drew sounded exasperated. "It's dark out. I'll be safer on the streets than you. For once, can we skip the argument? Just throw out the keys."

Caitlin glared at the closed door as she pulled her jeans over her hips. It was on the tip of her tongue to tell him to get lost, but he was right. Darn it. She yanked the zipper up with more force than necessary. A woman alone on any city street after dark wasn't smart. She'd dealt with enough rape victims at the crisis center to know better.

"Come on, Catie. Be reasonable. Give me a little credit for being concerned about your safety."

"All right. Just a minute." She found her keys, returned to the door, and opened it.

Drew was leaning against the doorjamb, arms crossed over his chest. She was highly conscious of his endearing smile and the way her heart began a slow hammering.

She lowered her gaze. A jade sport shirt was tucked neatly into a pair of jeans as old and worn as hers. Glancing up again, she noticed how the color of his shirt made his eyes even more impossibly green. He was clean-shaven, recently showered and groomed, and too darn appealing for *her* peace of mind.

"The keys?" he prodded her, holding out his hand.

Embarrassed to be caught staring, she quickly dropped the key ring onto his palm, then looked away for a second. When she glanced back, she discovered him viewing her shirt with a great deal of amused interest.

"Nice bulldog," he said, nodding toward the University of Georgia logo.

She looked squarely into his half-shuttered eyes. "Bulldogs can be dangerous creatures. When provoked, their bite can be quite vicious."

He reacted to her veiled warning with a slow appraisal of her entire body. "Even the most vicious beast can be tamed if a man has the right touch."

"Touching the beast is a good way to lose a finger or two." She crossed her arms over her UGA bulldog. "Are you going after my car or not?"

"Okay, I'm going. Be back in a little while." He grinned flippantly, then added, "Don't worry. I'll be careful with your precious Nellie."

Startled, Caitlin demanded, "How'd you know I call her that?"

"The day little Bobby Webster and I were playing catch and *accidentally* dented the hood"—Drew congratulated himself for working his innocence into the conversation—"you screamed that I'd killed your poor Nellie."

Renewed ire sprang to life in Caitlin's eyes, changing them to molten gold. An excellent time to depart, he thought, but couldn't resist chucking her under the chin as he turned away.

Drew walked down the hallway. He could almost feel her glare accompanying him. When he reached the foyer, he heard her slam her bedroom door.

Grinning, he left the house.

•   •   •

Drew ran down the European-narrow street. He loved the sense of freedom he got from running. Loved it almost as much as he loved living in the Garden District. He felt he belonged there every bit as much as the antebellum homes, sprawling oaks, magnolias, and lush subtropical vegetation.

He smiled as he passed a house similar to his. The rectangular shotgun cottages, with rooms arranged directly one behind the other, had been popular in the 1800s. The theory of the design amused him. Supposedly, a shotgun could be fired through the front door and pass out the rear door without hitting anything. He'd bought his house when he was a med student at Tulane and had worked hard over the years to renovate it. The small cottage was his pride and joy, a peaceful haven in times of trouble or sorrow.

All too soon, he reached Napoleon Street and the end of his run. He located Caitlin's VW wedged between two pristine status symbols, a Porsche and BMW. To say the vehicle she lovingly called Nellie had seen better days was a gross understatement. The little car was a battered and bruised lady dressed in a torn-and-worn gold gown.

Drew chuckled as he unlocked the door and got in. Caitlin's loyal attachment to her decrepit VW both amused and impressed him. He would count himself fortunate indeed if anyone ever offered him the kind of fierce loyalty she bestowed upon this hunk of scrap metal.

It took him a couple of tries to get the engine started. Thinking of ways to entice Caitlin out of her room that night, he eased out into the street.

Why he was so intrigued by a woman who considered him a clown was a mystery to him. Maybe he'd been alone too long and just needed companionship. Maybe he'd simply lost his mind.

Although both he and Caitlin were completing their residencies at Riverview Hospital, he really didn't know her very well. Pediatrics and obstetrics occasionally interacted, but his path didn't often cross hers. When he'd heard through the hospital grapevine a month ago that her apartment building was being sold for condos and she needed an afford-able place to live, he'd jumped at the chance to take her on as a housemate. He'd hoped doing so would give him an opportunity to get to know her better. So far, all he'd succeeded in doing was irritating her.

Halfway home, he was struck by a brilliant idea for making peace with her. He made a sudden U-turn and headed for the nearest video store.

Caitlin threw a worried look at her bedroom clock. Drew had been gone for forty-five minutes. She estimated the time it would take to walk, run, or crawl to Napoleon. None added up to that length of time.

What if he'd been mugged? A knot of anxiety tightened in her chest. She paced to the window and toyed with the curtain.

He could be hurt. Pivoting, she crossed the room.

He could be dead. She felt sick.

Then her eyes narrowed. Maybe he was just joyrid-ing in her car!

She planted her fists on her waist. If he wasn't lying mugged or dead somewhere, she'd kill him for worrying her like this!

She stalked over to the vanity table and sat down. Needing to get her mind off the mental image of his broken body slumped over the steering wheel, she began rearranging things. She put away a pair of pierced earrings, shifted a glass lamp several inches to the right, then moved it back again.

With a finger, she traced a crystal and silver perfume bottle. It was one of her mother's periodic "fluff" gifts. She picked it up, opened it, and dabbed a little perfume on her wrist. Definitely fluff, she decided, sniffing the exquisite scent. Designed for enticing the opposite sex.

Caitlin grimaced. She could almost hear her mother saying, "For heaven's sake, darling, there's nothing wrong with having a man to share your life with."

Ellen MacKenzie had given up a promising opera career to marry Caitlin's father and had never regretted her decision. She was happily married and wanted the same thing for her children, especially her only daughter.

Her mother's constant reminders of that in the form of fluff gifts frustrated Caitlin. Not that she had anything against marriage. It simply didn't seem to be in the cards for her.

She'd love to have it all, Caitlin freely admitted to herself. A career, someone to love, and perhaps a family someday. But she knew from experience that wasn't likely to become a reality. The divorce rate was alarmingly high for people in her profession. All too often, she'd seen her colleagues emotionally devastated after spouses or lovers walked out of their lives.

Her own one and only serious relationship had failed too. She'd met and fallen in love with an ambitious, idealistic, young legal eagle during her last year of medical school.

Caitlin jumped up and strode into her adjoining bathroom. Turning on the sink faucet, she began scrubbing the perfume from her wrist as she remembered the last few painful months with Adam.

At first, Adam had sworn he could take in stride her long hours of hospital work and studying. He'd claimed to understand her determination to work harder than anyone else to win top honors on each rotation. It hadn't taken him long, though, to resent all the time she devoted to her work rather than to him. Their relationship had deteriorated rapidly. When it finally came down to hard choices, neither of them had been able to give the other enough. In less than a year, he'd left her for someone who met his needs and expectations.

Caitlin turned the water off and dried her hands. The experience hadn't soured her on relationships. But it had shown her it would take a very special man to handle her demanding profession. She wasn't sure such a man existed, and she couldn't settle for less in that area of her life any more than she could compromise on what she wanted in her career.

Where were those memories coming from? she asked herself in annoyance as she walked back into the bedroom. The fluff gifts, she supposed. Or perhaps it was her crazy, mixed emotions about Drew.

Drew. Unable to stand not knowing what had happened to him, she grabbed her purse and stalked out into the hall. Halfway down the corridor, she suddenly stopped to consider what she was doing.

Going out to look for him was dumb. He could be anywhere. She chewed on her lower lip. Call the police? What would she tell them? Her lunatic housemate had her car and *might* be dead or hurt?

A sound caught her attention. A key scraped the front door lock. Relief washed over her. It was quickly followed by irritation.

Drew entered the house and closed the door behind him. When he looked up, he saw Caitlin stalking toward him as if she were ringleading the righteous indignation of a thousand saints. The way her chin jutted out reminded him of a bulldog just dying to bite his ankle. He smothered a laugh. Yes, sir, he had trouble right here in Crescent City.

"Going somewhere?" He looked pointedly from the handbag slung over her shoulder to her shoeless feet.

"Daniels!" she exploded. "Where the hell have you been? Wipe that smirk off your face." She smacked him lightly on the arm. "Do you have any idea how worried I've been about yo—" Her lips clamped together.

Drew realized with delight she'd almost admitted she'd been concerned about him. It gave him a warm feeling. If he counted on one hand the number of people he knew who actually cared enough about him to worry, he'd have quite a few digits left over.

"Your car?" he prompted. Confusion momentarily clouded her eyes. He grinned. "You were worried, I take it, about poor Nellie?"

She flicked her hand at his arm again. "Of course. why would I worry about your sorry hide? Of all the stupid, thoughtless, crazy"—she punctuated each word with a finger poked into his chest—"irresponsible, stupid, thoughtless—"

"You're repeating yourself." He caught her hand, stuck a videocassette into it, and forced her fingers to close around it. "How 'bout mean? Nasty? Rotten is good."

She frowned at the brown plastic cassette box. "What's that?"

"It's a videotape," he said, unable to resist the obvious comeback. Then he quickly added, "It's a peace offering. I'm sorry you were worried, but I had to go to two stores to find it."

She didn't say anything; she merely stared at him.

"Look, I honestly wanted to do something nice for you. How about giving me the benefit of the doubt?"

He imagined the thoughts racing through her head. Is it a joke? Open the box and Jack pops out.

Paper snakes. Perhaps creepy crawly things. *Trust me*, he said with his eyes while knowing she had no reason to do so.

Caitlin gazed searchingly at him, then looked down at the video. She didn't know what to think or what feeling to believe. A part of her wondered where the punch line was hidden. Another part felt inordinately touched and pleased.

Slowly, she turned the cassette over to see the title on the spine. "*Dark Victory*," she read aloud.

She sounded as surprised as Drew had hoped she'd be. He smiled warmly. "I know you like Bette Davis movies."

"I do," she said, glancing up. "But how did you know?"

He looked into her puzzled eyes, enjoying the way the colors blended and shimmered in the light. "Last week, I saw you watching one on the late show."

"I don't remember you coming into the room that night." A curious sensation began fluttering in Caitlin's stomach. She shook her head as if to dispel the disquieting feeling.

Drew left off his intense study of her eyes as her hair caught his attention. He liked the way it billowed out with the slight movement of her head, then resettled gracefully about her face and shoulders. He also noticed her hair smelled like apple blossoms.

Ordering his runaway thoughts to behave, he cleared his throat. "Uh, I just stood in the doorway for a moment. You were so absorbed in the movie, I didn't want to disturb you. I hope you like *Dark Victory*. Have you seen it before?"

She smiled slightly. "Oh, yes. A dozen times."

He tried unsuccessfully to hide his disappointment. "Then you probably don't want to see it again."

"Wrong! I love it. It's one of my favorites. I never tire

of seeing it." Her smile intensified, sending out a blinding radiance.

Heavens to—to—Nellie, he thought, as he struggled for an appropriate description of her smile. He came up with *killer*. The eyes, the hair, the smile. Drew decided he was in a lot of trouble.

"Great," he finally managed to say. "Want a sandwich to go with your movie?" Way to go, bozo, he admonished himself. If he couldn't stun her with his wit, feed her. His mind was definitely running amok.

"Sure. I am a little hungry." She sent out another one of those smiles guaranteed to cause him so much trouble.

He smiled back. "You set up the VCR, I'll make the sandwiches. Ham and cheese okay with you?"

"Sounds good." She headed for the living room, then stopped to glance at him over her shoulder. "Are you going to watch it with me?"

"You bet." Whistling, he turned toward the kitchen.

If there were a race for preparing sandwiches, Drew knew he could be a contender. That is, he amended, if neatness didn't count.

He returned to the living room carrying a plate and a fistful of napkins, a can of soda tucked under each arm.

Caitlin was curled up on the sofa, staring into space.

"Help," he said. "Take the drinks. My armpits are freezing."

She laughed and rescued him.

He sat down and settled the plate on the cushion between them. "Have a sandwich." He scooped one up for himself and took a bite.

Caitlin studied him for a moment, wondering why she should feel so nervous when he appeared completely at ease. He was acting as if they were the best of buddies. Maybe he'd kissed her on impulse and had already forgotten about it, and she was simply creating something to worry about.

Deciding to put the whole thing out of her mind, she helped herself to a triangle of bread filled with thinly sliced ham, cheese, and lettuce.

They ate in silence until an awkward need to start a conversation enveloped her. "By the way, thanks for going after my car."

"You're welcome." He met her gaze. "I'm glad you accepted my peace offering. Things are going to be different now. I like having you for a housemate, and I want you to be comfortable here."

"Well, thank you." What did he mean by *different*? she wondered. "After living in an apartment, it's nice being in a house again. Your home is lovely."

He smiled proudly as his gaze swept over the room. "Thanks. You should have seen how neglected and run-down it was when I bought it. It took me a couple of years of hard work to make it into a real *home*."

She picked up on the almost reverent tone he bestowed on the word home. It raised questions in her mind because it didn't fit her image of him. "Did you do any of the work yourself?" she asked curiously.

"I learned to refinish hardwood floors and repair cracked walls and ceilings. Plumbing and electrical wires were beyond my capabilities, but I did most everything else. It was worth every minute."

She looked at him for a long moment, mulling over this new revelation. Her perception of him was undergoing a series of changes, she realized. The practical-joking clown part of him was the most visible. But she was slowly coming to suspect a great deal more went on beneath his painted surface.

"Shall we start the movie?" he asked.

Mentally storing the new discoveries he'd revealed, she nodded. As Drew turned on the TV and VCR with the remote control, she settled back against the sofa, smiling in anticipation at once again seeing one of her favorite old films.

When Bette Davis appeared on the screen, he exclaimed, "Look how young she looks!"

Caitlin absently murmured, "Uh-huh."

"She isn't exactly a beautiful woman," he continued thoughtfully. "But there's something about her that radiates sexuality. It's the eyes." He nodded. "Oh, yeah. One smoldering glance across a crowded room from those eyes and a man knows he's been vamped. Her eyes remind me of—" Drew broke off, realizing he was about to blurt out *yours*. He stuffed the last bite of sandwich in his mouth.

"Bette's got what our grandparents' generation called *It*," Caitlin said.

"I like that." Did Catie know she had *It*? he wondered.

She frowned at him. "Are you going to talk through the whole movie? I hate it when people do that."

"Sorry. I'll be quiet. You won't even know I'm here." Trying to make good on that promise, he turned his attention to the TV.

He tried to get into the film, but couldn't. His thoughts constantly strayed to the woman sitting within arm's reach. The scent of apple blossoms filled his senses, driving him crazy. Tension coiled deep within him. He wanted to reach out and thread his fingers through her hair, then repeat the explosive kiss they'd shared earlier.

"Have you ever been in love?" he suddenly asked, startling them both.

"What?" She gave him an exasperated look.

He patiently repeated the question.

What in the world did he want to know that for? she wondered. "Once," she admitted grudgingly. "At least, I thought I was."

"I've never been in love. What happened with you and the guy you thought you loved?"

She sighed. "You said you would be quiet."

He grinned unrepentantly. "I really want to know. Tell me and I'll shut up."

"Okay. He dumped me for a woman who wanted to get married and give dinner parties. End of story."

Drew eyed her speculatively. She didn't sound like she was still hung up on her old flame. "Don't you want to get married someday?"

"You sound just like my mother," she muttered.

His brows furrowed. "What have you got against marriage?"

His tone reeked of disapproval, setting her teeth on edge. "Not a thing," she snapped. "Do you mind not talking? I'm trying to watch the movie."

"Fine." Drew laced his fingers together over his stomach. "Watch the damn movie." What was her problem? he wondered. Marriage was sacred. When he found the right woman, he'd marry her in a heartbeat. And unlike some of the people he worked with, his marriage would last forever. Trading partners like used cars didn't appeal to him.

He sneaked a peek at Caitlin. Her stiff posture told him she was angry. What was she really mad about? His talking during the movie? Her having to admit to being dumped? Or the subject of marriage? He shook his head. Women. To his dying day, he'd never understand them.

He stood up abruptly. "I'm going to bed. My on-call duty on pediatrics starts at six."

"Good night," she said without looking at him.

Her curt dismissal irritated him. Simply reacting, he leaned down, planted his hands on her shoulders, pulled her to her feet, and kissed her.

Too surprised to protest, Caitlin went completely still. After the first shock wore off, she relaxed and began to participate, her lips softening and parting under his. Just as she was getting into it, he lifted his head and let her go.

"Good night," he said, and left the room.

Caitlin flopped back down on the sofa. The man kissed like a dream. But he was totally crazy and talked entirely too much.

Her concentration was fractured. She was keenly aware of Drew's absence. It took a major effort, but eventually she became caught up in the movie again.

All too soon came the scene where Better Davis's character realized she was dying. That part always got to Caitlin. Tears streamed down her cheeks in sympathy.

"Catie?"

She looked up. Drew stood beside her. She hadn't heard him reenter the room. Swiping at her eyes with the back of her hand, she decided the man needed a collar with a warning bell.

He sat down next to her, murmured something, and handed her a handkerchief.

Embarrassed, she mopped up her tears, then blew her nose loudly. "Oh, Lord!" She reached for him, clutching a fistful of his shirtsleeve. "Can you believe she's going to let her husband go away without telling him it's the end?"

Though he knew she was only reacting to the movie, Drew couldn't stand to see her cry. It made something inside him ache. "It's all right, Catie." He wanted to kiss her tears away and bury his face in her apple-blossom-scented hair.

He settled for putting his arm around her shoulders, and was pleased that she didn't pull away. "It's okay. It's only pretend. Remember Bette Davis lives to be Baby Jane," he said, trying to lighten her mood.

Caitlin instinctively leaned into his embrace. Nice, she thought, as his arm tightened around her. Underneath, Drew Daniels was one nice guy. "I know." She dabbed at her eyes again. "This scene just gets to me."

He muttered under his breath.

"What did you say?" she asked, glancing up at him suspiciously.

"*Doom* and *gloom*. Next time I'm getting a Tom Hanks flick. I'll take comedy over this stuff any day."

She glared at him. "*Dark Victory* is a classic."

"It's depressing. I can't believe you prefer to cry than laugh."

"Daniels, there's more to life than pratfalls and one-liners."

His eyes widened in mock horror. "There is?" He looked as if she'd just told him the Easter bunny was a fraud. "I'm crushed."

"Shut up." She elbowed him in the ribs. "Bette's dying. Show some respect."

This time he managed to remain silent until the final credits. When the movie was over, he picked up the remote control and hit the rewind button.

Caitlin sighed. "That was wonderful."

No longer emotionally involved with the tragic story, she suddenly realized she was cuddled up next to Drew. She was surprised at how comfortable and companionable she felt with him at the moment. It had been a long time since she had allowed herself the simple luxury of snuggling against a man's warm, solid body. She'd almost forgotten how good it could feel.

In a way, this closeness made her a bit shy. She glanced up at him beneath her lashes. "I thought you went to bed in a snit."

Drew grinned. He loved the way she left herself open to puns and misplaced modifiers. "I don't own a snit. If I did, I certainly wouldn't wear one to bed." Mischief sparkled in his eyes.

Oh, no. Caitlin could see the nice guy slipping into his clown mode. The whoopee cushion stage couldn't be too far behind.

"In fact . . ." He paused, and the grin grew wider. "I prefer to go to bed in my birthday suit."

Three

It was hot the next morning, even before dawn. Mist covered Riverview Hospital like a veil, lending eerie dignity to its benevolent gray lady appearance. The large teaching hospital, located by the Mississippi River near the heart of New Orleans, buzzed with activity while most of the city still struggled awake.

At 6 A.M., Caitlin arrived at the obstetric/gynecology unit and was thrown into an emergency situation. A patient she had often seen in the free clinic had been in labor all night. Now the young woman was exhausted, and the fetal monitor indicated her unborn child was in distress.

The patient's name was Diane Pierce, and she was not yet out of her teens.

"Call it," Caitlin instructed a nurse.

The labor nurse pushed a button on the wall that sent out an emergency signal.

"Diane," Caitlin said gently, smoothing damp brown bangs from the young woman's forehead, "we're going to give you oxygen. Don't fight it. Try to breathe normally. Your baby's heartbeat is a little low. That tells me the baby is in some kind of distress and we need to do something about it. The oxygen will help. In a moment, we're going to take you into the delivery section." She kept speaking quietly and calmly as she arranged the oxygen mask over Diane's face, all the while praying she was worthy of the trust she saw in her patient's eyes.

Soon the room was filled with emergency personnel. An anesthesiologist took over Caitlin's job of monitoring the oxygen.

She looked at the young woman's husband. Joe Pierce stood holding Diane's hand. His face was ashen. He was not much older than his wife and just as scared. "You may come with us or wait outside," Caitlin told him.

"I want to be with Diane. I promised," he said in an unsteady voice.

As Diane was wheeled to the delivery section, Caitlin took Mr. Pierce with her to scrub. When they were scrubbed and gowned, they entered the delivery room.

"Fetal heart ninety-eight," someone called out.

Caitlin took her place at the table and let her training take over. Time took on a new dimension. She was aware of everything going on around her, yet her world was confined to the urgency of the impending birth. As the assisting resident continued to monitor the fetal heartbeat, Caitlin concentrated on instructing Diane to push with the contractions. Soon the baby's head crowned, and after one last push from Diane, Caitlin held a tiny infant in her hands.

"It's a girl," said the assisting resident.

A murmur of collective sighs went around the group but Caitlin did not join them. Coldness settled in the depths of her stomach. Healthy babies were blue when delivered. The Pierce baby was pallid and limp.

Working rapidly, she clamped and cut the umbilical cord, then suctioned out the infant's nose and mouth. Exchanging a worried glance with her assistant, she moved away and he took her place to finish the delivery.

Caitlin quickly carried the motionless baby to a table on the far side of the room. She placed a tube into the newborn's trachea that connected with the larynx and bronchial passages. The infant girl's chest rose as a machine squeezed oxygen into her tiny unused lungs.

Hardly daring to breathe herself as she worked, Caitlin prayed for a sign that the baby was capable of breathing on her own. In some distant corner of her mind, she heard an anguished wail from the mother.

Someone appeared at her elbow. "I'm from pediatrics."

Hearing Drew's voice, she glanced up. Relief flooded through her. Although she'd never worked with him before, she knew his reputation as a brilliant pediatrician.

She saw recognition in his eyes, then his gaze lowered to the still infant. "Brief me."

She rapidly told him how the baby's heart rate had dropped and explained what they had done in response.

He nodded, then picked up a sterile stethoscope and placed it on the newborn's chest. "One ten," he said, relating the rising heart rate. "She's beginning to pink up a bit. That's a good sign. Keep giving her oxygen. When her heart rate's at one twenty, we'll give her a chance to breathe on her own."

They worked together silently. To Caitlin it seemed to take forever for the baby's heart rate to reach the safe margin. When it did, she watched Drew gently remove the tube. She stared down at the tiny chest, willing it to rise and fall.

"Breathe. Come on, angel," Drew whispered. "You can do it. Breathe, angel."

Nothing happened. He replaced the tube.

With iron control, Caitlin reined in her emotions. "Will you take over?" she asked. Although she wanted to stay with the baby, her primary responsibility was to the mother.

He nodded without looking at her, and she returned to her patient.

After making sure there had been no complications with the afterbirth and assuring Diane and Joe that their baby would be fine, she hurried back to Drew.

"Heart rate's up. One forty," he said, briefly glancing at her.

Hope rose in Caitlin's breast. One forty was normal.

Suddenly, the infant flexed her legs. Her diminutive arms flailed, fighting the tube.

Caitlin wanted to laugh, cry, blow her cool image with a lively dance. Most of all, she wanted to grab the boy wonder of pediatrics and kiss him silly in gratitude.

"That's it," he said triumphantly. "We've got a good baby." He took the tube out again, and the infant gulped in air. "Welcome to the real world, angel."

Drew's angel let out one loud cry of indignation. The entire room went still. Another infant howl broke the silence, followed by cheers, laughter, and applause from the emergency staff and the parents.

Someone shouted, "Hot damn, that's beautiful noise!"

Drew smiled down at the infant. "It certainly is," he murmured, delicately stroking her cheek.

He glanced up at Caitlin. She stood close beside him. Her eyes were suspiciously moist and softly glowing. "Catie." She blinked, the focused on him. "Nice work," he told her. "If you hadn't gone into action at the first sign of distress, this little girl could have been in serious trouble."

"Thanks." Her eyes relayed the warm smile hidden behind her surgical mask. "It's frightening how rapidly a fetal heart rate can bottom out. Do you think she'll be all right?"

"You bet she will." He picked up the baby and cradled her in his arms. A nurse handed him a sterile sheet, and he wrapped it around the furiously squalling child. "Let's show her to her parents, then I'll take her up to the Intensive Care Nursery for a complete check and observation."

The young parents greeted them with tear-streaked faces and wide smiles. Caitlin introduced Drew. He answered their timid questions and explained the baby's immediate care. When he finished, he asked them what they were going to name their daughter.

A silent consultation passed between the Pierces. Seeming to reach an unspoken agreement, Diane said shyly, "We're going to name her Caitlin Andrea for Dr. MacKenzie and you. But we'll call her Catie."

Drew followed their gaze to the woman beside him. She gasped, her eyes widening with surprise. He grinned. "Catie," he said as she glanced at him, "is a fine name."

Later that morning, Caitlin stood at the fifth floor obstetrics/gynecology nurses' station, sipping strong black coffee and hoping the caffeine would kick in soon.

Her on-call duty had started off on the run with the Pierce delivery. Only four hours into her thirty-six-hour shift and she already felt exhausted. But just knowing little Catie Pierce was sleeping peacefully in the Intensive Care Nursery made her feel good.

She had been impressed with the way Drew had handled the situation. His reputation was well deserved.

Smiling sleepily, she thought again of how the Pierces had named their daughter for the two of them. It was a first for her, and she wondered if it was for Drew as well. She'd ask him about it the next time she saw him.

"Caitlin Andrea," she murmured, testing out the names. Funny how well they fit together. And stranger still, she felt as if an irrevocable connection had been forged between her and Drew by having a tiny scrap of humanity bear their names.

Her eyelids grew heavy. Holding the cup between her hands, she leaned against the counter, allowing herself to slip into lassitude.

"Ah-a! Asleep on your feet again. Wake up, kiddo!"

Caitlin lurched forward. She opened her eyes to see Debbie Wilson, the morning supervisory R.N., grinning at her from the other side of the counter. "Just resting my eyes," she said, smiling sheepishly.

"Sure, kiddo." Debbie's pretty café au lait face reflected her good nature in an ever-present smile. Intelligent eyes, so brown they sometimes appeared black, twinkled with amusement. "I've heard that one a million times. You residents and interns make lousy dates. The last one I went out with dozed off twice between the soup and salad courses."

"Remind me not to ask you out," Caitlin said.

"You're not my type anyway. I heard about the Pierce baby. Congratulations."

"They named her for me and Dr. Daniels."

Debbie smiled. "Nice feeling, huh?" She ran a critical eye over Caitlin. "You look awful. In fact, you look worse than my cat." She paused for dramatic effect. "He *died* last month."

Caitlin laughed and raised her cup in a salute. "That's what I like about you, Debra Jo. Always handy with a compliment." She swallowed the last drop of coffee.

"I call 'em as I see 'em." Debbie plucked the empty cup from Caitlin's hand, then marched around the counter the way she marched through life—sure of herself and capable of anything. She went to the coffee urn and poured them both another dose of the steaming liquid.

"Sit down before you slide onto the floor," she said, pulling out a desk chair for Caitlin. "Might as well be comfortable while you're waiting for the vultures. You'll need your strength for pumping and priming the fresh batch of medical students and interns."

Caitlin sat down and gratefully accepted the cup her friend thrust into her hand. Debbie perched on the edge of the desk as if ready to fly off at a moment's notice.

"I always dread the first day of rotation change," Caitlin admitted. Every three months she was given a new team of interns and students to supervise as they rotated through the various disciplines at the hospital. "Especially the students. They're so competitive, it's frightening. They'll do anything to show one another up for honors."

Debbie nodded sympathetically. "Hell of a way to start off a perfectly good Thursday." She blew on her hot coffee, then took a cautious sip. "One of the residents on the third floor warned me we're getting a real stinker this time. The guy's name is Paulsen. I understand he has an attitude problem. He's an intern with a surgeon fantasy." She rolled her eyes. "You know the type."

Caitlin buried her face in her hand and groaned.

"Just great. I recognize the name. Paulsen's on my list."

"Too bad," Debbie said. She drank her coffee in silence for a moment, then asked, "So, kid, what's with you this morning? Your day's hardly begun. You usually make it through to the thirtieth hour before—"

"Turning into a clone of your dead cat?" Caitlin finished with a smile.

Debbie chuckled. "Right. What's the matter with you? Your darling Dr. Daniels still playing tricks on you? What'd he do this time? Hide your panty hose in the freezer?"

Caitlin's smile faded. The twinge of possessiveness she felt at Debbie's teasing words startled her. "Do you really think he's . . . you know?"

Debbie laughed. "Kid, either you need glasses or your libido needs an overhaul. The good doc is drop-dead gorgeous. Half the female staff would die to be in your moccasins."

"He's just my landlord," Caitlin said. Her tone was defensive, though, and she mentally kicked herself.

"Wake up and smell the formaldehyde, kiddo. He's a landlord who occupies the same house. One who looks at you like you're the best-looking thing on the dessert cart."

"He does not," Caitlin insisted.

"Does too." Debbie grinned. "This conversation ought to be taking place in kindergarten. Seriously now, I've never seen you act so nervous about a man before. Makes me curious."

Caitlin refused to rise to the bait. "Curiosity and big trucks are the top-rated cat killers. Maybe that's what happened to yours."

"You're no fun at all," Debbie complained. "Always keeping everything to yourself. I—Uh-oh." Her eyes widened. "Don't look now, but here he comes."

"Who?" Caitlin turned to look.

Debbie hopped down from the desk. "If he asks you out, say yes." She grinned as Caitlin scowled at her, then strolled away.

With a sense of dread mixed with anticipation, Caitlin turned to watch Drew boldly stride toward her. The power of his presence shook her composure.

"Good morning," he said cheerfully.

"What are you doing here? Is something wrong with the Pierce baby?"

"Nothing's wrong with our little Catie." Drew smiled, liking the way that sounded. "We're going to keep her in the ICN to run a few more tests, but I don't expect any complications. I didn't mean to scare you by showing up without warning. Just thought I'd come by and talk to you for a minute."

"Oh, well, that's nice."

He noted the wariness in her eyes, as well as the shadows beneath them. "You look tired. Didn't you get any sleep last night?"

"I slept like a baby." Her gaze flickered away briefly, and she locked her hands together in her lap.

"I didn't sleep very well," he admitted. "I kept dreaming about cream pies and kisses that knocked my socks off."

"Daniels!" Caitlin quickly checked the area to see if anyone was listening. "This place has a thousand ears. I'd rather not broadcast that unfortunate incident to the world."

The smile on his face evaporated. "I don't think of last night as an unfortunate incident. I rather enjoyed it."

Caitlin saw hurt flash in his eyes, then wondered if she'd imagined it, because it was gone so quickly. During the past few weeks, she'd come to realize Drew Daniels was awfully good at keeping a happy clown face painted over his true feelings.

She let out a sigh. "Don't you guys on pedies have anything to do?"

"Oh, sure," he said, taking Debbie's place on the edge of the desk. "We've been having a trivia contest. It's been going on for a week. Think fast. Who won the 1959 World Series?"

"I have no idea and I don't care." She gave in to the need to laugh—something she was finding much easier to do since meeting him. "Is that what you came to talk to me about?"

"No." He picked up a pencil from the desk. "I wish you'd laugh more often, Catie. It makes me feel good."

A shiver coursed down her spine. No one had ever said that to her before.

He tried balancing the pencil on his finger. It wobbled precariously. "Will you have dinner with me tonight?"

Caitlin sat back, unconsciously creating more space between them. "Thank you, but no. I don't think it would be a wise move right now. It would be best if we kept our relationship strictly on a friendship basis."

Absently twirling the pencil between thumb and forefinger, Drew studied her closely. "Don't friends eat together?" he asked.

"Yes, but—" She suddenly felt vulnerable and far too open under care careful scrutiny. "Drew, don't rush me."

Like most people in his profession, Drew was attuned to reading between the lines. He recognized the hint of uncertainty in her voice, and he instinctively knew that was something she didn't often reveal. Her wariness also told him she was as interested in him as he was in her, but she didn't feel in control of the situation. He could understand that. Control was something he also valued.

"You understand what I'm saying, don't you?" she asked.

Her tone, the look in her eyes, asked for reassurance that the chemistry flowing between them could be confined within the bounds of friendship. He'd be lying to them both if he told her that.

Stalling for time, he replaced the pencil, positioning it exactly as he'd found it on the desk. "You're very stubborn, shrimp bait," he finally said, keeping his tone light.

"Catie, I mean, Caitlin!" She gritted her teeth. Now he had her using that nickname, yet she simply couldn't afford to see herself as the soft, warm person "Catie" projected. But it was preferable to "shrimp bait." She sighed wearily. "You make me crazy."

"The feeling's mutual," he murmured. He reached out and tucked behind her ear a strand of hair that had escaped from her braid. "Can you feel it?"

"What?" she asked, though she knew. It was the remembrance of awakened passion.

"The magic."

She shifted away from him. "Go take care of a sick child. My team will arrive for rounds in a minute."

The magic seemed to retreat as he stood up. "That's right. It's rotation day. Good luck with your neophytes. Keep the turkeys in line."

Caitlin watched him walk away, uncertain if it was relief or regret she felt.

He'd almost cleared the nurses' station when he stopped and looked at her over his shoulder. His sensual mouth curved into a smile. "See you at dinner."

Before she could form a protest, he was gone.

Still thinking of Caitlin, Drew stepped off the elevator onto the pediatric unit. Someone called his name, and he looked down the corridor. Mark Gordon, a big, freckled-faced, sandy-haired man came lumbering toward him.

"Yo, chief, gotta case right up your alley."

"Good morning, Mark," Drew said, taking the patient chart the second-year resident held out to him. "Tell me about it."

"First admittance. A five-year-old boy exhibiting symptoms of leukemia. Free clinic referral."

To the casual observer, Drew gave the impression of only mild interest. Inside, his complete attention was focused on this new case.

"Kid's name is Joey Anderson," Mark continued. "Youngest of six children in a single-parent home. His mother brought him in. We've got him in the charity ward for now. The bloodsuckers are doing a work-up."

The two men discussed the case until they entered one of the children's wards. Several kids immediately demanded Drew's attention. He paused to smile and speak to each one, then followed Mark to an area partitioned off by curtains.

The boy looked pale and rather lost lying on the hospital bed. A technician stood on one side of him drawing blood samples, and a harried-looking woman in a faded print dress that hung on her too-slender frame stood on the other side. Between absent pats on the child's shoulder, she darted worried glances at her watch.

Mother and son glanced up as Drew and Mark approached the bed.

Drew quickly assessed the boy. He appeared small for his age. Thick golden curls haloed his cherub's face, and something in the child's expression touched a chord in Drew's heart. Perhaps it was the boy's effort to show the world a brave front, although a tear hung suspended on one of his lashes. Or maybe it was the impression of fragility in his unusual sapphire eyes.

Drew smiled and received the merest reflex of the child's lips in return.

Then fear crept into the boy's gaze. Drew was all too familiar with that reaction. He knew to a new patient he was just another white-clad person, which meant more poking, prodding, and pain. Again, he smiled warmly, allowing the empathy he felt to come through.

He gave the chart back to his colleague, then slipped his hand into his pocket and palmed a stick of sugarless gum. "Hi, Joey." Drew raised his hand in greeting, letting the gum slide down his sleeve. "I'm Dr. Daniels, but most of the kids call me Dr. Drew. Do you like magic tricks?"

The child nodded, though his fear hovered in his eyes like a shadow.

"I know a few tricks," Drew went on, "but I always need help with the magic words. Do you think you could help me say them?"

"Guess so," Joey said.

"Good." Drew lifted his arms and wiggled his fingers. "*Credo quia absurdum*," he chanted, a Latin phrase that meant; I believe because it is absurd.

The child solemnly repeated the words.

Drew showed his empty hands, then reached down to pull the stick of gum out of the little boy's ear.

A gleam of wonder chased away the fear. Small fingers closed around the silver wrapper, and an angelic smile spread across Joey's face.

Drew ruffled his blond curls. The battle was on, and he intended to win.

It was a little after ten P.M. Activity had settled down on the ob/gyn unit. Caitlin's team of students and interns had scattered to study or grab a bite to eat, and for the first time since she'd come on duty, she was alone in one of the empty visitors' lounges.

She sat by a plate glass window, staring out at the lights twinkling on the black velvet river and listening to the steady sound of rain pummeling the glass. Though she was exhausted mentally and physically, her mind simply refused to shut down. It kept whirling away, sifting through a jumble of thoughts and emotions, returning more frequently than she liked to Drew Daniels.

Earlier that evening, she'd watched the clock with dread and anticipation, expecting Drew to show up for dinner. He hadn't shown or called.

"Okay, so I was an idiot for waiting for him," she muttered, frowning up at the ceiling. The cracked plaster didn't answer. She felt just as cracked for talking to the ceiling. She also felt like a woman who had been stood up. What she needed was a clown to cheer her.

Caitlin sighed softly. The previous evening she'd convinced herself she could handle her hormones. But after two sensational kisses, one restless night, and a day during which her thoughts strayed too often to Drew, she wasn't so certain.

Friendship, she reminded herself firmly, was the only thing she could afford to feel for him. Her residency at Riverview would end in July. The next step toward her career goal of going into infertility research meant relocating to another state. Establishing a long-term relationship under the circumstances was out of the question, and she simply wasn't interested in a casual affair.

Perhaps it would be best if she found another place to live. Caitlin closed her eyes and rubbed her aching forehead. But where would she go? She'd already pounded the sidewalks, inspected every available apartment in New Orleans. The undeniable truth was her budget didn't stretch far enough to make anything decent a viable option. She was in debt with college and medical school loans that would take her the next ten years to repay.

Yet knowing how Drew Daniels rang her chimes, could she safely tough it out until July? Nine months and two weeks was a long time to live under such a strain.

Maybe she was worrying about nothing. Maybe she was just too tired to think clearly. She decided to go to the dorm for residents on call and take a quick nap. Perhaps things would be different after a few hours of rest.

Caitlin headed for the dorm. Halfway there, along a quiet hallway of patients' rooms, she was startled by the sound of someone crying. She stopped outside a semiprivate room and listened.

Tortured sobs rose in crescendo. She looked at the room number and remembered that both occupants were private patients. Ward and charity admissions were the complete charge of residents and interns, but her responsibility for private patients was defined and limited.

Caitlin placed her hand on the half-shut door, palm flat, fingers spread.

The crying faded.

If she chose, she would walk away, stop by the nurses' station, and ask an R.N. to check on the patient.

The anguished sound began again. Something twisted inside her. Caitlin pushed the door open and entered.

"Can't you do something about her?" came an adolescent whine out of the darkness. "I was here first. How am I supposed to sleep with her freaking out like that."

"Count rock stars," Caitlin advised, walking past the first bed and on to the second.

Taking a small flashlight out of her pocket, she switched it on.

The woman was curled up in a fetal position. The IV attached to her hand was stretched as far as it would go. Her body shook violently.

Caitlin checked the IV while she recalled what she knew about this patient.

Kerry Ledet. Thirty years old. Admitted for emergency surgery. Ruptured ectopic pregnancy in the left fallopian tube. Right fallopian tube and ovary excised from a previous ectopic.

Struggling to remain detached, Caitlin remembered assisting Mrs. Ledet's physician in surgery that afternoon. The damage had been beyond repair, and the left tube had been removed. Her fingers trembled as she switched off the flashlight and returned it to her pocket.

"Mrs. Ledet," she said, gently touching the patient's quivering shoulder. A strangled cry of rage and grief rent the air, joining the audible whines still coming from the next bed. "I'm Dr. MacKenzie. Are you in pain?"

No response. Caitlin tried again. "Is something wrong? Do you need medication for the pain?"

Still no response. She wondered if the distraught woman was even aware of her presence.

"Go away!" The low reply was almost lost in a hoarse sob. Kerry Ledet struck out with her fist.

Caitlin caught her hand and held on when the woman tried to pull away. "Calm down. You'll rip out the IV. Everything is going to be all right."

As soon as the words left her mouth, she regretted them. A wave of helplessness enveloped Caitlin. Of course everything wasn't going to be all right. The woman's hope of having a child of her own had been surgically removed. Kerry Ledet probably felt nothing would ever be all right again. Logical or not, Caitlin felt her part in the procedure weighing her down like a sin.

She stood there in silence, feeling inadequate. Such intense grief was difficult for her to deal with. Nothing she could say or do could take away the inner pain of the soul.

Time passed. She held on to Mrs. Ledet's hand, trying to absorb the hurt.

Eventually, the sobbing became intermittent gasps, then stopped. She felt the woman's body relax into a natural slumber. For a moment, Caitlin stared into the darkness, feeling as drained as if she, too, had cried herself into exhaustion.

She gently released Mrs. Ledet's hand, then rearranged the bed linens around her.

Alone in the residents' dorm, Caitlin lay in the dark on one of the half dozen cots. She'd seen too many women like Kerry Ledet, devastated by infertility problems. Tonight's incident confirmed she'd made the right decision to further her training and go into infertility research.

Someone entered the room and turned on the overhead light. "Hey, Mac, you asleep?"

The voice grated on her ragged nerves, and she threw her arms over her eyes. "Not anymore, Dr. Paulsen."

"In that case, you won't mind if I keep the light on to read," said the intern who had rotated onto her team that morning.

She heard him flop down on a cot, and she slowly opened her eyes, blinking to adjust to the brightness. She turned her head to look at him.

His tall, lanky form barely fit the small bed. She

watched him light a cigarette, focusing on his graceful, fine-boned hands. The hands of a surgeon. He inhaled deeply, then opened the book.

Caitlin was reminded of a Modigliani painting every time she looked at Paulsen. His wide-spaced blue eyes were set in a long, sharply angled face. He was a thin bundle of energy, always moving in an awkward, almost adolescent fashion. Even at rest, his feet rapidly wagged to and fro like a friendly dog's tail.

That comparison made her smile, because there was nothing remotely friendly about him. The intern's personality was abrasive, bordering on cranky. He'd lost no time in telling her first thing that morning what he thought of the ob/gyn service. From there, the day had gone downhill.

Caitlin looked away. She knew she had better set a few ground rules with Paulsen. If she didn't, his negative attitude would affect her entire team and destroy everyone's morale.

"Hey, Mac."

And the first thing she needed to do was disabuse him of the notion that he could get away with calling her "Mac." "You will refer to me as Dr. MacKenzie," she said firmly.

"Yeah, right. Dr. *Mac*Kenzie. Ever get any real action on this minor league service, or is it always this boring?"

Caitlin met his gaze. The little twerp wore a smile like an insult. She speared him with cold eyes. "You've crossed the line of insubordination several times today, Dr. Paulsen. Don't do it again. While you're on my team, your days will not end and the work will rarely stop."

His angular face took on the expression of a recalcitrant child. "I'm not interested in being a baby-catcher. I'm going into surgery. This rotation is a waste of time."

Caitlin sat up. "You don't have to like the ob/gyn service or me. However, I am your supervisor for the next three months. I expect your cooperation and courtesy."

His eyes flashed like quicksilver, but he wisely remained silent.

"You will adjust your attitude," she continued, "or have it adjusted for you. Every morning you will check on your patients' primary care an hour before grand rounds. On grand rounds you will be questioned for interpretations, diagnoses, and complications. I expect you to be prepared to answer those questions or you will soon be shown how very little you really know. Am I making myself clear, Dr. Paulsen?"

The intern leaned down to stub out his cigarette in an ashtray on the floor. "Crystal clear, Dr. MacKenzie." He snapped his book closed, got up, and left the room.

Too tired to get up herself and turn off the light, Caitlin settled back onto the cot and closed her eyes.

Almost immediately, she heard the door open once more. Paulsen returning for round two? Oh, no, she thought. "I'm warning you," she said, keeping her eyes shut tight. "Be quiet and let me sleep or I'll deck you with a bedpan."

"Hold your bedpan. I come in peace."

Four

Caitlin jerked upright as she recognized Drew's low, cultured voice.

He stood in the open doorway, smiling. The warmth and intensity of that smile rattled her. Earlier, she'd wished for a clown to cheer her up. Now he was here, and she felt ridiculously, dangerously happy to see him.

She kept her expression carefully blank. It was an art she'd perfected over the years. "Why are you here?"

Drew hid his disappointment over her less than enthusiastic greeting. "I promised you dinner." He hooked his thumb into his belt. "Is it safe to come in? You won't deck me if I do, will you?"

"It's too late for dinner," she said, remembering how she'd waited for him earlier that evening. She reminded herself, also, of her intention to remaining aloof.

But he looked so good, she was having a difficult time holding on to her resolve. His white lab jacket hung open, revealing a crisp pink shirt, dark gray trousers, and—she looked closer—a colorful fish tie. He appeared fresh, bright-eyed, and incredibly sexy. In comparison she felt disheveled, knowing her braid was coming undone and her clothes were rumpled.

If she were smart, she'd tell him to get lost, but she wasn't feeling that sharp tonight. Nor could she bear the thought of sending him away. "Oh, come in. I won't hurt you. I've already bagged my limit today."

His laughter rippled the air. He crossed over to the cot and gazed down at her in an intimate way that sent a shiver along her spine.

"Have you had dinner yet?" he asked, while noting that the circles under her eyes seemed twice as dark as they'd been that morning. She looked as if she needed a hug and eight hours of sleep. He would happily supply the hug, but didn't think it a wise move at the moment.

She shook her head in answer to his question.

"Then it isn't too late," he said. "I have a pizza waiting for us in the other room." He held out his hand to help her rise.

The moment she put her hand in his, Caitlin experienced a dizzy rush of feeling. Either her imagination was playing tricks on her or the air really was sizzling with electricity. She swung her legs over the side of the cot and quickly stood up.

He didn't let go of her hand immediately. Their gazes locked. In his eyes she saw a longing so deep and intense, it bore into her soul. She wanted to wrap her arms around him and hold him tightly. She didn't, though, because she knew it wouldn't be enough and it wouldn't be prudent to offer more than she could afford to give.

Drew felt her withdrawing from him emotionally. He released her hand and stepped back. Painting on a smile, he asked, "By the way, what kind of animal does one hunt with bedpans?"

She laughed, and he felt the tension between them evaporate. "It's open season on snotty interns."

"Ah, yes," he said with a nod. "I've bagged a few of those creatures myself." The teasing light left his eyes, and his forehead wrinkled in a frown. "Seriously, is someone giving you a hard time?"

"Nothing I can't handle." She slipped on her shoes.

He gazed steadily at her. "Are you sure?"

Her chin went up. She glared at him.

"All right." He raised his hands in surrender. "I'm sorry I asked. I'm certain you could handle the Middle East crisis single-handed. I didn't meant to annoy you."

"But you do it so well."

He raked his fingers through his hair. "It isn't intentional. Can't we have a simple conversation without antagonizing each other?" He offered her an engaging, peacemaking smile.

She looked up at the ceiling, then back at him. "Has it ever occurred to you that we might have an unresolvable personality conflict?"

"No." He didn't believe that any more than she did. Just holding hands with her a moment ago had generated enough heat to burn a hole through him. It frustrated him that she refused to acknowledge the obvious and potent attraction between them.

"The pizza is getting cold," he said, and gestured toward the outer chamber. "I'm going in there to eat it. Feel free to join me."

He wheeled around, walked to the door, then stopped. "My mother told me a gentleman always brings a lady flowers." Turning back to face her, he appeared to pluck a bouquet of garishly colored paper flowers out of the air.

Caitlin's lips parted in amazement. She automatically caught the bouquet when he threw it to her.

"We don't have a personality conflict, Catie. We're

attracted to each other. The problem is we don't know each other well enough to know what to make of it."

"That's absurd," she said without conviction.

He merely smiled, then closed the door behind him.

Drew had just polished off his first slice of pizza when the door opened. From his peripheral vision, he saw Caitlin standing in the threshold. She hesitated for a moment as if engaged in some internal debate.

He suspected she didn't know whether to hold out the olive branch of peace or smack him with it. Reaching for another slice, he ignored her. He'd made enough overtures. The next move was hers.

She started forward, each step purposeful, yet full of grace. Her face betrayed no clue to her thoughts. She seemed composed and reserved as usual. Her gaze swept over him, then lit upon the elegant black-and-gold box from Guzzo's Italian restaurant.

"We peasants usually make due with C.O.D. Pizzeria," she said, sitting down across from him. "I didn't know Guzzo's delivered."

Ah, he thought, the olive branch disguised as a safe topic. He wiped his mouth on a napkin. "They don't."

"You're on call tonight. I can't believe you'd go AWOL for a pizza." Her eyes were filled with skepticism.

"You wouldn't believe what I'd do for a Guzzo's pizza," he said grinning.

She scooped up a thick slice and bit into it as if she wished it were his jugular vein. After a moment, she asked, "Are you going to tell me how you acquired it or not?"

"I bribed an off-duty orderly to bring it back. Not only did I have to buy him dinner, too, I had to pay him another thirty for his trouble." Drew picked up a black olive that had fallen off his slice and popped it into his mouth. A teasing light shone in his eyes. "You know, you're the orneriest woman I ever shelled out ninety bucks for."

She blinked. "You were robbed."

"It was worth it."

Her head tilted slightly, and she gazed at him with a puzzled expression. "You use money so casually. It doesn't seem to mean anything to you."

"Do I?" He shrugged. "I suppose I do. It bothers you, doesn't it?"

"Yes. I'm still paying off med school loans and living from one paycheck to the next. A ninety-dollar pizza seems a bit on the extravagant side to me."

"Okay." he sighed dramatically. "I confess. I'm supplementing my meager resident's salary by ripping off cases of thermometers from the supply room. I sell them at street value to hypochondriacs."

He glimpsed a smile quivering on her lips, but she managed a frown. He had to hand it to her. The lady certainly had control.

"Put a cork in the comics, Daniels. If you want us to get better acquainted, you'll have to be serious sometimes." She picked up an unopened can of diet cola. "Is this for me?"

He nodded. "Please note it's your average vending machine beverage. Even us decadent rich folks make concessions now and then."

This time she did smile at his concession pun. "How very prudent of you. Rumor has it your family's in the steel business. Are you one of the decadent rich?"

"Unfortunately, I don't have time to be decadent." He helped himself to another slice of pizza. "I guess you could say I'm financially sound. My accountant always seems happy to see me." He hesitated for a moment, then continued, "My late grandfather used to be in the steel mill business when steel was king in Birmingham, Alabama. My father wasn't interested in the business, and the mills were sold before I was born. My father lives off his trust fund and investments. He spends most of his time in Europe and Palm Springs. We aren't on the best of terms."

Caitlin recognized both the false note of humor in his voice and the flash of sadness in his eyes. Apparently, the estranged relationship with his father hurt him. She felt a stab of sympathy for him, knowing how she would feel if she no longer had her close-knit family's love and support.

With anyone else, Drew would have felt the need to keep the conversation going. But with Caitlin, even silence was companionable. He didn't feel she expected further explanation about his family or needed him to entertain her.

He turned his attention to her hair, enjoying the way the red-gold strands gleamed in the light. She wore it twisted in the prissy braid she favored for work. On her the style appeared cool and reserved, like the persona she maintained. A few wayward strands clung to her temples and nape, though. One corner of his mouth quirked upward as he cheered them on in their bid for freedom.

"Is something wrong?" she asked, peering at him.

"No. Why?"

"You're looking at me funny. Do I have sauce smeared on my chin?"

"No. I was just admiring the view." He was rewarded with a disbelieving grin.

"This morning," she said, "Debbie Wilson told me I look worse than her dead cat. And *you* told me I look tired. I doubt I've improved much since then."

"Rough day?" he asked.

"I've had better." She wiped her fingers on a black-and-gold-edged napkin.

"Tell me about it," he urged. "I'm a good listener."

Caitlin's discipline wavered. The clown who plagued her so was missing tonight. Drew looked sincere, stripped of polite fictions and willing to give her his undivided attention and genuine interest. Perhaps it was the warmth of his smile, or the new layers of him showing through, but she was conscious of a desire to take a small risk in opening up. She found herself wanting to share the day's events with him.

She began slowly by telling him about Craig Paulsen and her concern that the intern's negative attitude would jeopardize the team's morale.

Drew asked a few questions, then suggested she assign Paulsen to assist her in surgical procedures as often as possible. "Letting him feel you have confidence in his abilities could make a difference in his attitude," he said. "Talk to him. Find out what's bugging him."

Thinking it over, she realized his advice was sound. When she'd decided to join him for dinner, she hadn't expected to dump her most pressing work problem in his lap. Nor had she expected him to hand back a viable solution to that problem.

She was so accustomed to holding everything inside, keeping her own counsel, that she'd forgotten how good it could feel to share even the most trivial dilemma with someone. Encouraged by that feeling, she related the incident with Kerry Ledet and how inadequate and helpless she'd felt in dealing with the woman's traumatic grief.

Drew braced his arms on the table. "Catie, you're too hard on yourself. You're not a psychologist. Faced with that kind of raw emotion anyone would feel inadequate. For what it's worth, I think you did the only thing you could. You held her hand and let her know she wasn't alone."

A slow smile spread across her lips. "You're a good listener. Thank you. Would you like coffee? Or do you need to get back to pediatrics?"

"Coffee would be great. I don't have to rush off just yet."

She pushed her chair back and stood up. As she started to clear the table, Drew caught her wrist.

"I'll clean up if you'll get the coffee."

"Okay. You use cream, don't you?"

"Yes, thank you." He smiled, obviously pleased she remembered.

Caitlin walked over to a square table against one wall, which held a coffee urn, coffee supplies, and an odd assortment of snacks. She filled two cups with coffee, spooned powdered creamer into his, then added some to her own because the brew looked a bit strong.

When she finished her task, she found Drew had taken a seat on one of the two green vinyl sofas. He'd made himself comfortable by propping his feet on the scarred coffee table in front of him. "Be careful," she advised, handing him a cup. "I think this brew may have more bite than a Doberman. No telling how long ago it was made."

"I'm used to drinking it strong enough to eat through a bank vault."

She kicked off her shoes and sat down, tucking one leg beneath her. "How are things on pedies?"

"Hoppin'. We had a great wheelchair race this afternoon." He smiled at her startled expression. "Some of the staff challenged the mobile kids. It was more of a relay race. The kids loved it. Catie, a couple of kids who've barely said a word or cracked a smile since being admitted were laughing and cheering on their team. I wish you could have been there."

His pleasure sparked a renewed vitality in her, edging out her weariness. She was surprised at how comfortable she felt with him. When he wasn't playing the clown, he was good company and easy to talk to. She didn't even mind that he called her Catie.

"Sounds wonderful," she said. "I can't believe the things you people get away with. Nothing like that ever happened on the pediatric service I interned on in Atlanta." She took a sip of coffee and found the brew potent but drinkable. "What else happened today?"

Drew began telling her stories about various children and their reactions to his amateur magic tricks, never realizing the different side of him Caitlin was beginning to see. As he spoke she caught another glimpse of the man beneath the patter and nonsense. For the first time, she began to understand that as unorthodox as his methods might be, Drew possessed an uncanny ability for making sick, frightened children happy. With his pockets full of gum, toys, and magic tricks, he gave them a few hours respite from their fears. Anyone who took the trouble to look beyond the surface knew he was a warm, caring person.

In the middle of telling Caitlin about an enterprising little boy who'd ripped off a case of cartoon character Band-Aids and sold them to other kids for a penny, Drew noticed she'd stopped laughing in all the right places. Her face was a study in pensiveness. What had he said to bring on such a transition?

He fell silent, and her exquisite eyes met his. Drew felt himself being drawn into them. Was it his imagination or was there some nebulous sense of warm, sweet light flowing between them, as if they'd suddenly tuned in to the very essence of each other? The feeling was strange yet exhilarating.

Her eyes widened, then a look of caution crept into

her expression. She glanced away as if embarrassed.

Drew gave himself a mental shake. How long had he been staring at her? Obviously long enough to make her uncomfortable. "I hope I'm not boring you." He grinned sheepishly. "I tend to get a little carried away when I start talking about the kids."

Caitlin relaxed. For a second she'd felt off balance, lost in a swirling mist of . . . She refused to put a descriptive tag on whatever she'd just experienced. Smiling, she said, "Just the opposite. I like hearing you talk about the children. It's obvious you love your work. What are your plans after July?" That was the favorite topic of every resident nearing the end of his or her speciality training at Riverview.

"I'm going to set up my own multidisciplinary practice. I like the idea of combining a diverse group of specialists under a common practice." Excitement shone in his eyes and was echoed in his smile.

"Where do you plan to establish your practice? Birmingham?" She watched the light in his eyes extinguish, and realized she'd said the wrong thing.

"No," he said shortly, his smile dying. "I have no ties to Birmingham anymore. There's nothing and no one to go back to. New Orleans is home." His tone softened. "I've been here since my undergrad days at Tulane. I plan to live and work here for the rest of my life."

Caitlin thought about that for a moment. It told her two things. His family situation was more painful than he'd let on, and he was surprisingly locked into this city. She would have liked to question him further, but the quiet, controlled way he'd spoken and his vehement attitude dissuaded her.

She chose the safer of the two topics to pursue. "Sounds like you've fallen hard for *The Big Easy*."

"You bet," he said enthusiastically, visibly relaxing again. "As far as I'm concerned, it's the *only* place to live. There's something about this city that just gets into your blood. I feel like I belong here. Whenever I go away, I look forward to going home, like a kid looking forward to Christmas and the last day of school all wrapped up in one."

He tilted his head and smiled at her. "You probably feel the same way about going home to Georgia."

She shrugged. "I guess so. I miss the mountains sometimes. But to me, home is my family. It wouldn't matter where they lived."

He gave her a skeptical look. "Really? Did you move a lot when you were growing up?"

"I was born and raised in a small college town. Maybe that's why I find it kind of exciting to live in new places."

He shook his head. "Moving around doesn't hold any appeal for me. I'm settled here, and here I intend to stay."

His adamant tone still bothered her for some reason, and she changed the subject. "Are you planning to build a facility for your practice?"

His expression brightened. "I've got my eye on an existing structure. It's an old three-story brick house on St. Charles Avenue. The building is sound, and there's plenty of space for parking. And best of all, it's only four blocks from home. Very convenient for family life someday."

Drew had always struck her as a live-for-today kind of person, so she was surprised to discover how thoroughly he had mapped out the rest of his life. Another one of her preconceived notions about him crashed and burned.

"What specialties do you want to combine?" she asked.

"Pediatrics, ob/gyn, internal, and family practitioners, and maybe a psychiatrist. I've discussed it with a few people who are very interested." He offered her a sudden magnetic smile. "How about you? Want to go into practice with me? We make a great team. Look how well we worked together this morning with the Pierce baby."

Although he had spoken on impulse, the idea of a partnership with Caitlin instantly took shape in Drew's mind.

She returned his smile, but shook her head. "The only way I could afford a private practice is to be recruited by a community desperate enough to offer me financial backing. But, I must admit, if I was going to be a practitioner and could afford it, your offer would be tempting."

He frowned. "What do you mean *if* you were going to be a practitioner?"

"My interest in infertility research is stronger. I've applied for research/study programs in Houston, Los Angeles, Baltimore, Chicago, and a few other places where I can work and further my training at the same time."

"I see. You'll be leaving then."

That unnerving quiet control was back in his voice, and Caitlin glanced away. "When I moved in, I told you I would be leaving in July." A curious hollow feeling began to grow in the pit of her stomach. She thought she heard him sigh.

She was leaving New Orleans, Drew thought. His feet hit the floor, and he sat forward, looking into his cup and wishing it contained something stronger than coffee. He took a sip. The coffee was as cold as he felt on the inside. July was only a little over nine months away. Pressure built up in his chest.

He turned his gaze to her. She was sitting quietly, her expression unreadable. He glanced down and noticed how tightly she held her own cup. A lot could happen between now and July, he told himself. It was possible she could reconsider her options.

"Catie, we both have a couple of days off when our shifts end tomorrow evening. Would you go out with me? We could spend Saturday in the French Quarter. Maybe take in some jazz music later at Preservation Hall."

She nervously tucked a strand of hair behind her ear. "I don't know," she said, turning to look at him. "Today's been so full of highs and lows. And frankly, it may not be a good idea for us to try to be anything more than friends."

He held on to his easy smile with great effort. "There's nothing wrong with your judgment. Catie, I don't know what you're thinking or how you feel. But I believe we have the potential for something deep and lasting. Don't ask me how I know because I can't explain it to myself. It's just a feeling. I can't offer you a written guarantee that a relationship between us will work. All I can do is ask you to give us a chance."

Caitlin shied away from his intense gaze. He was looking for a permanent relationship, something she also wanted for herself. But she was leaving in July.

She suddenly felt her orderly existence pressing against her chest like a two-ton weight. After years of reining in her emotions in order to cope with her professional life, she now seemed to be drowning in them. Ever since meeting Drew, her capacity for lightness and impulsive joy had been seeping through the cracks like water through a broken dam. She didn't know how to stop it. She wasn't sure she really wanted to.

But she was leaving in July. Common sense told her not to get any more involved than she already was. The desire to ignore common sense was overwhelming.

"Drew, I—" She broke off as the beeper attached to his belt clamored insistently.

He turned it off, then reached for the phone on the

table beside him. "What's up?" he said to whoever answered. "Joey Anderson?"

Caitlin watched his face take on an alert and immediately involved expression. She knew he'd just slipped into his professional mode as quickly and as automatically as another man might slip into his shoes.

"Has his temperature spiked? Okay, I'll be there in a few minutes." He replaced the receiver.

"Trouble?" she asked.

"Possibly." He stood up. "Thanks for having dinner with me. I really enjoyed being with you." His smile was brief but warm.

"I enjoyed it too." She rose, intending to walk to the door with him.

Reaching out, he ran a fingertip over her cheek. "Have you made a decision about going out with me?"

She felt strangely hot and cold at the same time. "I still don't believe it's wise for us to get involved."

He moved closer, curving his hand around her neck and urging her to meet him halfway. "You're probably right. But I don't feel like being wise."

Neither did she, but old habits were hard to break. "Let me think about it, okay?"

"Well, at least that's something. While you're busy thinking, consider this." He leaned down and kissed her with a hunger that belied the gentleness of his touch.

It was a kiss meant to melt the thickest ice block of reason. Unable to resist the growing need within her, Caitlin responded fully kissing the corner of his mouth, running the tip of her tongue along his full, lower lip. His arms wrapped around her, pulling her into the heat of his body.

As the kiss deepened, she gave in to the explosive passion that had been building between them over the past month. Intense emotion and pleasure sent shock waves coursing through her.

Drew slowly released her. Grinning engagingly, he tugged on the braid hanging over her shoulder. "I have to go. Walk me to the elevator?"

Caitlin nodded, thinking she'd follow him to China if he asked right now.

Five

Two mornings later, Caitlin gradually awakened to the sensation of something soft and feathery tickling her cheek. Still half-asleep and disoriented, she brushed her hand across her face, then rolled over onto her stomach. She sighed contentedly and snuggled deeper under the sheet.

A whistling sound drifted into her subconscious. Frowning, she dragged the pillow over her head. Cool air touched her skin. She fumbled for the top sheet, but couldn't find it. Shivering slightly, she curled into a fetal position.

The soft feathery thing rubbed against the sole of her foot, and she jerked. Just a dream, she told herself. A sensory dream of home and of her brother coming in to wake her. "Go away, Stephen," she mumbled in protest.

"Come on, Catie, wake up."

The voice, seductive as black silk, penetrated the layers of sleep fog in Caitlin's mind. Recognition brought her awake by degrees. She lifted the pillow a few inches and peeked out.

On his knees beside the bed, chin propped on his forearm, Drew sat watching her. A smile spread slowly across his face, and its warmth rolled toward her like a heat wave. Her heartbeat quickened in response.

Embarrassment, annoyance, and pleasure swirled into one big mixed-up emotion. How long had he been there? she wondered.

"Good morning, sleepyhead. Who is Stephen?"

"My little brother." She lowered the pillow to cover her face again. "If I give you a quarter, will you go away?"

"Nope."

"Quarters always worked with Stephen."

The feathery thing touched the top of her thigh. She bit back a moan as it traveled the length of her leg to her foot. She kicked out in reflex, then reached for the hem of her football jersey, which had bunched up at the top of her thighs, and jerked it down to her knees.

"All right, landlord. This could be considered harassment." She pushed the pillow away and sat up. Glaring at him with narrowed eyes, she wondered how he could look so sexy this early in the morning. Well-worn jeans rode low on his hips. A white, unbuttoned dress shirt hung open, revealing a fine sprinkling of dark curling hair on his chest. The implement of torture he held in his hand was a daisy.

Caitlin finger-combed her tangled hair. "Didn't your mother teach you any manners? What are you doing in my room? This is *my* room, isn't it?" She made a show of checking out her environment.

Drew cocked his head to one side, studying her, taking in her tousled hair, the translucent quality of her skin, the smoothness of her legs. "You look sweet when you're asleep. Sort of cute and cuddly." And delightfully rumpled and sexy, he added silently. A flush tinged her cheeks as if she'd read his thoughts. "I was playing the prince waking Sleeping Beauty, but the princess turned out to be Oscar the Grouch."

She pointed to the door. "Out!"

He laughed. "Are you always grumpy in the morning?"

"Only when dopey landlords wake me up on my day off."

"You're getting your fairy tales confused. Dopey was one of Snow White's seven landlords. Lucky you, you only have one. Me."

Without comment, she crossed her arms and leaned back against the headboard. Drew was content just to gaze at her for a moment, enjoying the way her nightshirt stretched tight across her chest, molding itself to her small, perfectly shaped breasts. A part of him wanted to give in to the impulse to crawl into bed with her. But intellectually, he knew he wanted more, much more, than either of them were ready for.

"Then again," he continued, "maybe you're just feeling burnt out this morning. Working overtime can do that."

Caitlin frowned. Just before her on-call duty had ended at six o'clock the previous evening, another resident had called to ask her to cover for him for an hour. The hour had turned into four. It had been well after midnight when she'd finally gotten home, and Drew had already turned in for the night. How did he know she had worked late? "How do you know I wasn't out with a date?" she asked curiously.

"I called the ob/gyn unit."

Anger flared instantly. "You had no right to do that."

He held her gaze for a moment, then said quietly, "You're right. I have no excuse except that I was worried about you. When I drove your car Wednesday evening, I had a hard time getting it started. I imagined you alone in the parking garage, having trouble with it. I couldn't stand not knowing what had happened, so I called. I'm sorry."

Her anger faded. "Well, I appreciate your concern, but I prefer that you not do that again. If I ever need a ride home, I'll ask. Now, what are you doing in my room?"

"Waking you." He dropped the daisy into her lap, then stood up.

"Why?"

"You'll see." He walked out, leaving an aura of mystery clinging to the room.

Caitlin stared at the open doorway for a few minutes, wondering what he could possibly be up to. It was useless, and she gave up trying to imagine what new madness he could be concocting. The man was devious. His bag of tricks was bottomless.

She picked up the daisy and twirled the stem between thumb and forefinger. Drew was also as sweet as he was unpredictable. He'd worried about her last night. Smiling, she plumped her pillow, then located the sheet at the end of the bed and pulled it up to her shoulders. She lay down, holding the flower against her cheek. Complying with an inner demand, she closed her eyes.

She'd just begun to doze off when she heard the sound of cabinets being banged shut. Drew was in the kitchen, she thought. Then she heard him singing loudly. Whatever he was up to, she realized he wasn't going to let her go back to sleep.

Sighing, she sat up and propped the pillow behind her. She thought about getting dressed, but she was too comfortable to move.

"Got your eyes closed?" Drew asked from the hallway, staying out of sight of the open door.

"That depends. Is this one of your jokes?" she called back.

"What a nasty, suspicious mind you have, my dear." His tone of voice suggested indulgent humor. "I have a very nice surprise for you. Now close your beautiful eyes."

Did he really think her eyes were beautiful? She smiled. "Oh, all right. They're closed."

Bare feet slapped the hardwood floor. As he came near, Caitlin decided he'd either splashed on a very strange cologne or he was carrying bacon and freshly brewed coffee.

She felt the mattress dip slightly as he sat beside her. Something was laid across her lap.

"Surprise."

She opened her eyes and looked down at an antique wicker bed tray. Her gaze wandered over an elegant display of china, crystal, and silver. The dishes contained pancakes, bacon, chilled grapefruit, and coffee. A wine goblet was filled with orange juice. Another daisy lay beside the plate.

Not knowing what to say, she inhaled the smell of steaming coffee as though it would stimulate her frozen vocal cords into expressing appropriate appreciation.

"Catie. Do you like it?"

She raised her eyes. Drew was watching her closely. He wore a look of delight mixed with anxiety. She remembered seeing the same look on her brother's face when he was about five and he'd presented their mother with a jar he'd decorated with colorful macaroni. That unspoken need for approval shone in Drew's eyes. Did her approval matter so much to him?

"How wonderful," she finally responded. It was not only a comment about his effort to surprise her, but about the strangely complicated man himself.

His smile showed his pleasure at her words. As they gazed at each other, Caitlin felt everything else slipping away. There was only his smile, the oddly tender expression in his brilliant green eyes, and a sensation of lightness invading her body. She felt as if the bed tray covering her lap was the only thing keeping her from floating away.

Suppressing the strong urge to reach out and touch him, she glanced down. With a fingertip, she traced over the white wicker, feeling its rough woven texture. "Where did you find this lovely thing?" she asked, hoping to conceal the confused state of her emotions.

"In an antique shop on Magazine Street." He took a pale peach linen napkin from the tray and handed it to her. As she arranged it, he picked up the fork and cut into the generous stack of pancakes. "Open."

"I'm quite capable of—"

Laughing softly, he took advantage of her open mouth and fed her.

Swallowing the delicious morsel, she gestured toward the tray. "What did I do to deserve such special treatment?"

"Because you're crazy and kind enough to work other people's shifts. Or maybe I'm the one who's crazy." He hesitated for a moment, then added, "About you." Not wanting to make a big deal of that, he shrugged and held out another bite of pancake.

Her senses skyrocketed, robbing her of a reply, so she allowed him to feed her again. When she trusted herself to speak normally, she said, "You're a good cook. How do you manage to make such fluffy, round pancakes? Mine run all over the skillet and turn into flat whale-shaped messes."

"Thank you. The trick is to chill the batter before spooning it onto a griddle."

"No kidding. Never heard of that." She reached for the fork, but he moved it beyond her grasp. She gave him a questioning look.

"Did I mention this is breakfast for two?" he asked. "You have to share."

"Hey, as long as I don't have to clean the mess you no doubt made in the kitchen, I'm willing to share with you." She smiled at him. "You are a terrific cook, but the kitchen always looks like a war zone when you finish. Give me the fork."

"We culinary artists do not trouble ourselves over such insignificant details," he said loftily, placing the fork in her outstretched hand.

"That's for sure." She speared a generous helping and swirled the pancakes around in the syrup. Holding one hand underneath the fork to catch stray drips, she offered it to him.

He closed his hand over hers, guiding the fork to his mouth.

She was mesmerized by the slow, sensual way he took the food between his lips. A flame began to burn in the pit of her stomach. He reached for her other hand. Her eyes widened with pleasant shock as his tongue ran lightly over her open palm, licking the drop of maple syrup there.

As the flame inside her flared even higher, she realized she was like kindling ignited to life by his fire. His simple yet seductive action fanned the growing heat inside her to a raging fire.

She didn't resist when he took the fork back and fed her again. Each slow, precise movement he made entangled her in the sensuous web he spun around them. Food had never tasted so good. Eating had never been such a sensual experience. Without being aware of doing so, she suddenly realized they'd consumed half the food he'd prepared.

Still under his enchanted spell, she watched as his hand moved to the crystal goblet. He lifted it and drank. How perfectly his mouth was shaped, she marveled.

When he lowered the glass, he smiled slowly. Caitlin knew if she were standing, that smile would have brought her to her knees.

He leaned forward, touching the rim of the fluted glass to her lower lip. Eyes locked on his face, she drank, savoring the slightly exotic flavor of champagne and citrus.

She heard him whisper her name. Reaching up, she hesitantly laid her hand on the side of his face. He tipped the glass and she drank again while searching out each nuance of emotion in the green eyes staring back at her.

Drawing the goblet back, he turned it and drank from the same spot as she had. Watching him, Caitlin was struck by the ceremonious quality of sharing the drink with him. In an extraordinary way, she felt as if it were an act of bonding.

In that infinite moment, she became aware of a subtle shifting of their relationship. Something within her gravitated toward him like a flower turning its face to the warm sun. She realized Drew had been right when he'd called this thing between them magic. Magic was binding them together in this moment in time.

She smiled, finally allowing herself to feel the joy his presence engendered in her. The heated glance he gave her in response added another ember to the fire burning inside her. Lowering her gaze to his lips, she felt an overwhelming desire to feel them moving upon hers. She sighed, the sound a throaty, sensuous purr.

She removed the goblet from Drew's hand and returned it to the wicker tray. Her smile lingered as she saw his questioning look, his deliberate stillness.

Bringing her other hand up, she cupped his face, then leaned close to touch her lips to his. Lightly, she dragged her mouth across his warm, moist skin. The feel of him was all she remembered it to be and more. He tasted of champagne, citrus, and promises. Yet it wasn't enough.

Her internal fire soared higher, and she felt as light and weightless as the flames. His lips parted, inviting her in. She stroked his tongue with her own, saturating her senses with the demanding, passionate duel.

He gripped her shoulders, drawing her into a loose embrace with gentle strength. She slid her palms along the rough-smooth surface of his face, then slipped her fingers into the silver-and-sable hair at his temples.

Groaning, Drew broke away to rain kisses over her face. The ecstasy of being close to her was so rich, he wanted to prolong it for an eternity. He had to fight to keep from being dragged under by a tidal wave of need; the need to possess and be possessed so thoroughly that neither of them could think of ever letting go. Using his last vestige of common sense, he gripped her shoulders tighter, lifted his head, and sat back.

Startled by his abrupt movement, Caitlin stared into his eyes. Air became trapped in her lungs. He was looking at her in a way that made her feel like a rare, exquisite flower that bloomed just for him. For the first time in her life, she realized what an addictive thing it could be to appear so precious in a man's eyes.

Drew took in an unsteady breath. Her eyes glowed with an emerald fire. He recognized it as a signal of passion. The same change had occurred during their first kiss the night of the pie fight. He didn't think it would take much to push their relationship into the physical realm.

So why, he asked himself, wasn't he taking her up

on the invitation he'd felt in her kiss and now witnessed in her gaze?

Because if he wasn't completely knocked-for-a-loop mad about her, he'd eat his best red-and-blue stethoscope, clip-on stuffed koala bear, and all. And because he knew enough about her to realize she approached life cautiously, liking everything well thought out and neat. She would regret anything done in an impulsive moment and that was not what he wanted.

Serving her breakfast in bed had seemed a brilliant idea earlier that morning. Now he wasn't so sure. If he was smart, he'd exercise a little of her caution and get the hell out of the room.

He slowly released her, his arms falling to his sides. She smiled, drenching him in sunshine. He dropped his head into his palm and decided he was dying. One more killer smile from her could break his will.

"Catie, don't smile at me." He heard a thread of amusement in his voice and knew it stemmed from the absurdity of his predicament, which was of his own blasted making. "Tell me to leave right now. Because if I don't, I might crawl into bed with you and we'll never have that first date I promised you."

"That's okay by me. First dates are so awkward." Caitlin gasped. Surely she hadn't said that! "I mean—" Color stained her cheeks. "I don't know what I mean."

Laughing, Drew raised his head. She wasn't going to be any help at all. Where was her discretion when he really needed it? He realized there was no one to save him from himself except—oh, Lord!—himself. Using his grandfather Daniels's gruff tone and often repeated words, he silently ordered, *straighten your spine, boy.*

He got off the bed and stood military straight. "I will not be cheated out of a first date." He picked up the tray. "We're going to spend the rest of today having fun in the French Quarter. At the end of that date, I'll kiss you at the front door and ask you out again." A teasing grin lightened his expression. "Besides, I don't want you to get the idea I'm easy. I'm not that kind of guy."

She tilted her head back, looking up at him through a fringe of black lashes. "That's not what I've heard," she said.

He shook his head. "Ugly rumors. I'm chaste."

"Right, *chased* by everything in a skirt."

He grinned. She was quick with a comeback. He liked that. After putting the tray on the floor, he bent over her, grasping her arms. "I'm fleet-footed." He lowered his voice to a suggestive whisper. "But for you, Catie, I could be persuaded to slow down."

Caitlin closed her eyes, anticipating his kiss. Suddenly, she was dragged off the bed. Her eyes flew open as her feet hit the floor. She steadied her balance by holding on to one of his arms, which had quickly encircled her waist. "That was a rotten trick," she sputtered.

Holding her, Drew decided, was definitely a mistake. He let her go and stepped back. "Get dressed. We're going on that first date if it kills us."

Caitlin stared at him for a second. She'd invited him into her bed, and he'd refused. How mortifying. Yet on one level she was actually relieved. She was glad he'd had the good sense to stop them from jumping headlong into something they'd both regret.

He smiled at her, then picked up the tray and started to walk away.

Getting too deeply involved with him would be the dumbest thing she'd ever done, Caitlin thought. She was leaving in July. He was staying in New Orleans. She simply couldn't jeopardize her future by getting tangled up in a complicated emotional relationship. "Drew, wait," she called.

He turned back to her.

"I think we need to talk." She sat down on the edge of the bed, lacing her fingers tightly together.

"Oh, no," he said. "You've got that serious look in your eyes. You've talked yourself out of spending the day with me, haven't you?"

When she nodded, he set the tray beside the door. Slowly, he walked back and sank down on the end of the bed. "Why?"

She looked away, unable to meet his steady gaze. "You're right about this thing you call the magic between us. It's pretty overwhelming. A few minutes ago, I was ready to drag you into bed with me and say to hell with everything. I've never felt that way with anyone else."

"I know. Scary, isn't it?"

"Yes, it is." She managed to look him in the eye. "I don't get involved in casual relationships, and anything more permanent simply wouldn't be fair to either of us. You know I'm leaving New Orleans when my residency ends."

Frustrated and discouraged, Drew ran his fingers through his hair. "Catie, let me get this straight. You're worried about getting emotionally involved with me. You don't want your heart broken. Okay, I can understand that. I don't particularly want mine broken either. The simple fact that we're having this conversation tells me we're already involved on an emotional level."

He held up his hand to stop her forthcoming protest. "Let me finish. You told me you've applied for research positions in several different places. Okay, but just because you've applied doesn't mean you'll be accepted. What are you going to do if you aren't?"

"I will be accepted," she said coldly. "If not this year, then next year. I want it as much as you want your multidisciplinary practice. I didn't just wake up one morning and say, gee, I think maybe I'd like to do research work. I made that decision a year ago after careful consideration."

He slid closer to her and took her hands between his. "You have to decide what's best for you. But there's something very strong between us. All I'm asking is that you give it a chance. Spend some time with me. You set the pace, and I'll follow."

Her heart fluttered. She knew she should back away from any kind of relationship with him. Drew was an unexpected element in her life. An exciting, irresistible force. And heaven help her, she didn't want to resist.

"All right," she said, hoping she wasn't making the biggest mistake of her life. "I'd like to spend some time with you. But please remember, it doesn't change the way things are."

He could accept that for the time being. But she was wrong. As he'd assured himself a dozen times in the past two days, a lot could change between now and July. "Okay, let's start with our day in the French Quarter. Let me show you how wonderful this town really is."

"I've been here over two years," she said dryly. "I've seen everything this city has to offer. So if you're thinking I'll fall in love with it and not want to leave—"

"But you haven't seen it with me," he quickly interrupted. "Come on, Catie. This is N'awlins', dawlin'. The city *care* forgot. Let's go out there and show 'em we don't care either!"

She smiled at his pep-rally tone. "Okay. But this isn't a date. We're just two friends spending the day together."

"Whatever you say." He released her hands, and stood. It damn well was a date, he thought as he left the room. The first of many.

In record time, Caitlin was freshly scrubbed, powdered, perfumed, dressed, and staring at her reflection in the vanity mirror. Normally, she didn't pay much attention to clothes and makeup. Today, though, she'd put on one of her mother's more recent fluff gifts—a silk turquoise blouse. Together with a braided turquoise, black, and yellow belt and a straight knee-length skirt, it made a nice outfit. She added a thin gold necklace and gold hoop earrings, then slipped into a pair of black espadrilles.

Assessing her reflection once more, she frowned, thinking she looked like she was dressed for a date. "It's not a date," she said firmly. After glancing in the mirror one last time, she headed out to find Drew.

She found him lazily draped over the sofa in the living room, reading a book and listening to the stereo at full volume. He'd changed into pleated khaki trousers and a white cotton T-shirt under a loose, unbuttoned tropical print shirt. His canvas deck shoes, worn without socks, were spotlessly white. She smiled. He looked like an Ivy League man with a Gauguin fantasy.

Moving quietly, she walked over to the shelving unit that housed his high-tech compact disc and stereo equipment. The man had good taste in expensive toys, she thought as she lowered the volume.

He glanced up from his book. From the gleam of pure male appreciation in his eyes as his gaze slowly traveled over her, Caitlin decided her mother was right. A little fluff was good for the soul.

Caitlin leisurely strolled with Drew down Bourbon Street in the French Quarter. Although it wasn't quite noon, the area was full of tourists and natives. Music drifted out from the various establishments lining the street. Jazz, rock, lively Cajun syncopated rhythms, country, blues, and zydeco—a kissin' cousin of Cajun music—mingled together and rose like heat off the sidewalks.

Fascinated by Drew's reaction to their surroundings, Caitlin kept darting glances at him. His face glowed with rapture, and his eyes seemed to be trying to see everything at once. He looked as happily awed as a kid on his first visit to Toys "R" Us.

"I never get enough of this place," he suddenly stopped to say. His gaze swept upward to the lace ironwork on the balcony of the building they were standing in front of, then back to Caitlin. "It's fantasy, reality, and one hell of an ongoing bawdy carnival. The past and present collide in a disorder so fascinating, you can't tell where one leaves off and the other begins. Somehow I wouldn't be surprised if I saw the pirate Jean Lafitte standing at the corner of Bourbon and Chartres, munching on a hot dog and passing the time of day with the *Lucky Dog* vendor."

He looped an arm around her waist. "Don't you love it?" he shouted, lifting her off her feet and swinging her around in a circle.

Laughing, she remained in his embrace even after her feet touched the ground again. To her the Quarter simply represented tourists in search of the ultimate good time, bars and strip joints, and shops whose wares ranged from tawdry to sublime. But seeing it through Drew's eyes, it took on a new dimension. Everything around her became vibrantly alive with color and feeling.

"Yes," she finally responded, "I love it."

"Then what are we standing here for? Let the good times roll." He grabbed her hand. "Let's go get crazy."

Caitlin laughed again for the sheer joy of it as she followed him into a novelty shop.

She was still laughing when they came out of the

store. "Okay. Tell me the truth." She shook her head vigorously. "Is it really me?"

Drew lowered his gigantic rhinestone-encrusted sunglasses and peered consideringly at the *Thing-A-Bob* stars on the long springs attached to the band on her head. Pieces of silver-and-purple glitter fell into her hair as the stars bounced and twinkled in the sunlight. He nodded and shoved the glasses back up on his nose. "They're totally ridiculous. Definitely you."

She stabbed his chest with one finger, making him walk backward. "If you want to see ridiculous, you ought to take a look at yourself in those bug-eyed monstrosities."

Arguing playfully over each other's questionable taste in tacky souvenirs, they continued on down the street.

The next few hours were spent in exploring everything from the Old Absinthe House to Pirate's Alley. Sharing one of Pat O'Brien's famous "Hurricane" drinks in a to-go cup, they ran in and out of shops, then danced in the middle of Bourbon Street with the copper-faced boys who routinely entertained French Quarter crowds with their unique jazzy tap steps and eagerly accepted all donations for their efforts.

Over a lunch of seafood gumbo and crawfish etouffée, Drew learned that Caitlin had never been inside a voodoo store. Afterward, he took her to one, and they examined odd charms and amulets, all guaranteed either to cure the purchaser's every ailment, grant every desire, or confound an enemy. Just for fun, Drew bought them both a gris-gris that the priestess swore contained the power to get a lover, hold one, or throw one away.

Caitlin felt hot, tired, and slightly giddy with happiness by the time they decided to take a rest in Jackson Square. She plopped down on a grassy spot in the shade of a palm tree near the statue of Andrew Jackson. Slipping off her shoes, she stretched her legs out and leaned back on her elbows.

It was a perfect place to recuperate from the day's activities. Tourists swarmed in and out of the red brick Pontalba buildings on each side of the Square. Jugglers, mimes, and street musicians performed in front of the majestic St. Louis Cathedral. Artists surrounded the park with their carts and brightly colored umbrellas. Their pastel and oil paintings of French Quarter scenes hung on the park's ornate iron fence.

She smiled warmly at Drew, who sat facing her. "Thank you," she said softly.

Drew's gaze skimmed the length of her shapely legs, then he focused on her face. Did she have any idea of the sensual impact she had on him? he wondered as he smiled back. "For what?"

"For breakfast. For the best day I've had in a long time. For you being you." She laughed self-consciously.

"For teaching me how to act foolish again. I think I'd forgotten how."

He moved closer to her and reached for a strand of hair lying against her breast. He curled the silky strand around his finger. "Tell me, Catie, how do you feel about PDA?"

Six

"PDA?" Caitlin frowned as she searched her memory for the medical terminology of a newly discovered something. She came up blank. Not once had they discussed medicine all day, and she found she didn't welcome the intrusion of their professional lives. Nor did she like having to admit she didn't have any idea what PDA might be.

She sighed and shook her head. "I'm at a loss. Tell me what it is, and I'll let you know if I have an opinion."

He unwound her hair from his fingers and watched the strand float gently back to rest against her breast. "Public displays of affection." A slow grin spread across his mouth.

She grinned back. "Walked right into that one, didn't I? I thought you were talking about a new disease!"

"I think it is," he said, only partly joking. "And I've got it. My heart rate is skyrocketing. My palms are sweaty." He lowered his gaze to her mouth. "I'm dying to kiss you. So what's your opinion, doc?"

His eyes captivated her, stroked her like a caress. She noticed an increase in her own heart rate. And to her amazement, her palms felt moist too. Rational thoughts abandoned ship, except for one. The thought of pressing her lips to his.

She swallowed hard and forced herself to say lightly, "Take two aspirins, a cold shower, and call me in the morning."

"Wrong prescription." He laid his hand alongside her face, teasing the corner of her mouth with his thumb.

Caitlin remained motionless as panic and pleasure welled up inside her. She tried reminding herself not to get involved, but she didn't move a muscle as he lowered his head to hers.

He kissed her once, twice, then whispered her name against her lips. Her mouth flowed open, granting him sweet access. She reached up to weave her fingers through his hair, and the kiss deepened. Her whole body suddenly seemed unbearably sensitized.

Dragging his lips across hers, Drew turned his face and nuzzled her hair. "The worst part about PDA is the public part. Personally, I prefer private displays." He raised his head and met her desire-filled gaze. The glow of green fire singed him. His breath caught in his throat.

"Come here," he said, wrapping his hands around her arms. With her cooperation, he pulled her to a sitting position, then turned her to fit between his thighs, her back to his front. "Talk to me, Catie. Tell me about growing up in Georgia."

"Okay." Caitlin leaned against him, enjoying his warm solidity and the way his arms felt around her waist. She began by describing her family's log home, designed and built by her father, John.

Drew rested his chin on her head between the

Thing-A-Bob stars she still wore. He breathed in the apple blossom scent of her hair and listened to the beautiful sound of her voice. His eyes closed, and he saw the pictures she lovingly painted with her words.

He imagined the two of them sitting on the wide porch of the log house, drinking hot apple cider while watching the setting sun make the autumn-dressed mountains blaze with color. He could see John MacKenzie's harshly chiseled face and his gentle soul. Could smell the wood shavings and varnish in her father's workshop. Could see her mother, Ellen, a willowy blonde whose inner serenity shone from her china-blue eyes. He could hear Ellen's opera-trained voice as she sang with the church choir or as she worked over her quilting frame. He smiled when Caitlin told him how her brother, Stephen, nine years her junior and ten times her size, used to embarrass her in front of her dates.

"He's a junior at the University of Georgia," she added. "He's one of UGA's star football players."

"Did he give you the football shirt you wear a lot?"

"Yes," she said, and he could hear the affection in her voice. "He gives me one every Christmas. Stephen's predictable, but faithful."

"I'm an only child. I always envied my friends who had brothers and sisters."

She moved out of his embrace and sat facing him. "Now it's your turn. I want to know everything about you. What was your childhood like?"

It was on the tip of his tongue to respond with his usual glib answer. Talking about his childhood made him uncomfortable. He'd been one of the privileged from the day he was born, and had spent his early years in a house that deserved to be called a mansion. Everything a child could possibly want had been his. Everything, that is, except his parents' attention.

How could he explain a childhood filled with a soul-deep loneliness without sounding like a pathetic little rich boy?

Yet, he didn't want to tell her lies. Not when she was becoming so important to him.

Looking down at the ground, he plucked a blade of grass and rubbed it between his thumb and forefinger as he thought about a past he'd never tried to put into words before. "It was full of good-byes," he finally said.

The hollow sound of his voice cut straight to Caitlin's heart. "You don't have to talk about it if you don't want to," she said softly.

He shrugged. "It's no big deal."

But it was, she thought, watching a false smile mask his emotions. She had a feeling he'd learned early to use his sense of humor to keep unpleasantness at bay. "Why do you say it was full of good-byes?"

"My parents preferred to travel. Mostly in Europe." A distant tone crept into his voice. "In their social circle it was considered bad form to take children along. My parents and their friends were raised by housekeepers and nannies—British-trained nannies, of course—until they were old enough to be sent to boarding school for a proper education." The familiar mocking smile flashed briefly then was gone. "So was I. Until I was six, what I remember my parents saying most is, 'Good-bye, Andrew. Do try to be a good boy for Nanny and Mrs. Ellis.'"

Caitlin tried to imagine how he must have felt. Lonely and abandoned. She reached out to take his hand. Although it was a warm, humid day, his skin was cool. "Who is Mrs. Ellis?"

A genuine smile lighted his eyes. "Our housekeeper. She was a sweet lady. The nannies came and went, but Mrs. Ellis and my grandfather Daniels were the two people I counted on to always be there. She retired and moved to Florida to be close to her son's family after my mother died, and I was sent away to school."

"How old were you then?"

"Seven."

It was the last piece of the puzzle, and it brought the picture into focus for her, revealing why he seemed so determined to remain rooted in one place. "Did you like boarding school?"

He chuckled. "Make that schools. Before I reached the ripe old age of fifteen, I'd been politely requested to leave some of the finest prep schools in New England and a couple in London."

She hid a tremor of mild shock and more than a trace of sympathy. "Firecrackers under the headmaster's chair?"

"Once or twice." He laughed caustically, then continued, "Sometimes for being a disruptive influence. I was the class clown. Sometimes for setting a bad example by running away."

That made sense to her. Playing the clown garnered him attention, something he must have been starved for. But running away. She could only imagine how unhappy he must have been to do that. "Where did you go when you ran away?"

He squeezed her hand before letting go. "To my grandfather Daniels's house in Birmingham," he said, stretching out one of his long legs. "I'd show up on his doorstep, and he'd say, 'It's about time you got here, son. I'm sick of playing gin rummy by myself.' He was a ruthless old steel tycoon in his heydey. Taught me not to smoke by letting me make myself sick on one of his cigars. And he called me son."

Caitlin was struck by the wistfulness in his voice. She smiled. "You were very fond of him."

"I loved that old reprobate. He had a stroke and died when I was fifteen. That's when I stopped running away from school. There was nowhere else to go then. I've always regretted not being there to say good-bye to him and thank him for always taking me in."

"I'm sure he knew how you felt," she said gently. "Nana Rosamond, my maternal grandmother, is the only grandparent I can remember. She lived in Mississippi and rarely traveled more than fifty miles from home. Yet she came to my high school graduation ceremony. I never told her how much that meant to me, but I believe she knew."

Drew was silent for a moment, studying her, then he said, "You're easy to talk to, Catie." He'd told her more about his background than he'd ever told anyone before. "I have friends, but no one like you. I think you may be the best friend I've ever had."

Once again, she was surprised by this unpredictable man. "Thank you. I . . . I'm glad we're friends." She lowered her gaze. Smoothing a nonexistent wrinkle from her denim skirt, she was amazed that her hand trembled slightly.

When she glanced up again, she caught him looking at her as though he was trying to memorize every detail of her face. Her pulse quickened over that speculation.

"What about your father?" she asked. "Do you ever see him?"

Drew turned his head toward the river beyond the French Market. Funny, he thought, for a while he'd tuned out the sounds around them. Now he heard the mournful tune of a strolling saxophone player, pigeons cooing, the traffic on the street between Jackson Square and the French Market, and the foghorn blasts of ships passing one another.

Slowly he looked back at Caitlin. "I receive a royal summons once a year when he's in Palm Springs. We spend the weekend playing golf and wondering what to say to each other."

A wave of sadness hit her. Before she could say anything in response, he scrambled to his feet and held out his hand to help her rise.

"Let's walk," he said. "I want to stop by the antique clothing shop on Royal Street."

She nodded and put her hand in his.

As they walked in silence through the Square, Caitlin realized she'd experienced an incredible range of emotions since waking that morning. It was something she didn't often allow herself to do.

In order to deal with the emotional stress of her profession, she had developed a safety valve on her feelings, using it to shut off her emotions at will. With Drew, she was rapidly discovering that valve was faulty.

He served her breakfast in bed, kissed her like it was his last day on earth, and looked at her as though she were a rare orchid to be cherished. And now she'd shared his laughter and his pain. She had a terrible feeling she was about to dive fearlessly into a bottomless emotional sea. And the risk of drowning was very real.

She sighed and wound her arm through his. One day at a time, she told herself. Just take it one day at a time.

Good-byes were still on Drew's mind. When he felt her take his arm, he turned his head slightly to look at Caitlin. He loved her, he admitted to himself. Loved her warmth, her strength, the stubborn tilt of her chin, her elusive eyes, and the way she wasn't afraid to go after what she wanted in life. He loved the serious expression she often wore, and the logical way her mind worked. He even loved the way she was fiercely loyal to the wreck of a car she called Nellie.

A Magical World of Enchantment Awaits You When You're Loveswept!

Your heart will be swept away with Loveswept Romances when you meet exciting heroes you'll fall in love with...beautiful heroines you'll identify with. Share the laughter, tears and the passion of unforgettable couples as love works its magic spell. These romances will lift you into the exciting world of love, charm and enchantment!

You'll enjoy award-winning authors such as Iris Johansen, Sandra Brown, Kay Hooper and others who top the best-seller lists. Each offers a kaleidoscope of adventure and passion that will enthrall, excite and exhilarate you with the magic of being Loveswept.

- ♥ **We'd like to send you 6 new novels to enjoy—_risk free!_**
- ♥ **There's no obligation to buy.**
- ♥ **6 exciting romances—plus your _free gift_—brought right to your door!**
- ♥ **Convenient money-saving, time-saving home delivery!**

Join the Loveswept at-home reader service and we'll send you 6 new romances about once a month— _before they _appear_ in the bookstore!_ You always get 15 days to preview them before you decide. Keep only those you want. Each book is yours for only $2.25* That's a total savings of $3.00 off the retail price for each 6 book shipment.

*plus shipping & handling and sales tax in NY and Canada

Enjoy 6 Romances–Risk Free! Plus...
An Exclusive Romance Novel Free!

Detach and mail card today!

Loveswept

AFFIX RISK FREE BOOK STAMP HERE.

Yes! *Please send my 6 Loveswept novels RISK FREE along with the exclusive romance novel "Larger Than Life" as my free gift to keep.*

RD123   412 28

NAME

ADDRESS   APT.

CITY

STATE   ZIP

MY "NO RISK"
Guarantee

I understand when I accept your offer for Loveswept Romances I'll receive the 6 newest Loveswept novels right at home about once a month (before they're in bookstores!). I'll have 15 days to look them over. If I don't like the books, I'll simply return them and owe nothing. You even pay the return postage. Otherwise, I'll pay just $2.25 per book (plus shipping & handling & sales tax in NY and Canada). I *save* $3.00 off the retail price of the 6 books! I understand there's no obligation to buy and I can cancel anytime. No matter what, the gift is mine to keep–*free!*

SEND NO MONEY NOW.
Prices subject to change. Orders subject to approval. Prices shown are U.S. prices.

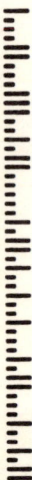

Was he setting himself up for the most difficult good-bye of his life?

Drew looked straight ahead. Putting his hand in his pocket, he touched a small cotton bag, the gris-gris he'd bought in fun.

To get a lover, hold one, or throw one away.

He knew what he would wish for if he believed. But he also knew no superstitious mumbo jumbo would hold Caitlin if she chose to go away.

At work on Monday, Caitlin took Drew's advice on handling Craig Paulsen. She allowed the intern to assist her in a major surgical procedure, and she was favorably impressed with his skills.

Afterward, she sat him down for a cup of coffee and a heart-to-heart. She discovered his negativity and offensive behavior stemmed from grief and anger over his father's recent death. The late Dr. Paulsen, a small town general practitioner, had wanted his son to follow in his footsteps. The young man was now stuck with a rotating internship he'd only applied for to please his father, and a load of guilt for wanting to chase after his own dream of being a surgeon.

Caitlin told him she understood how he felt, and promised to assign him to as many surgical procedures as possible. She let him know in return she expected him to improve his attitude.

By Tuesday, little Catie Pierce was ready to be released from the Intensive Care Nursery. With a great deal of pleasure, Caitlin placed the infant in her mother's arms. Standing back and watching the young parents with their tiny daughter, she was glad to see the open expression of love between these two teenagers. She knew they would need every ounce of that love to make it with the odds so heavily against them.

She checked on Kerry Ledet, too, who was healing physically but not emotionally. The woman's physician agreed with Caitlin about Mrs. Ledet's condition, and told her he'd already encouraged Mrs. Ledet to seek professional counseling to help her deal with her grief.

Caitlin saw little of Drew either at the hospital or at home most of the week. He was preoccupied with his new patient, Joey Anderson. The boy's tests results confirmed a diagnosis of lymphatic leukemia, and he was started on a protocol of treatment.

One of Drew's uppermost concerns was to prevent Joey from perceiving his necessary isolation as abandonment. Since Mrs. Anderson's financial situation prevented her from staying with her son, Drew sought her permission to line up volunteers to sit with the child day and night.

What free time Drew had that week was spent almost entirely on planning the Halloween party the pediatric staff was throwing for the kids. Drew was in charge of the event, which was only a week away, and there seemed to be endless meetings with various committees.

Although Drew easily managed to talk Caitlin into helping with the Halloween party, it wasn't as simple to convince her to go out with him again. It took him a week of coaxing, but she finally caved in. This time he made sure she admitted it *was* a date.

Friday evening, he reserved a private dining alcove at Winston's in the Hilton Hotel. He chose the restaurant because of its unequaled reputation for graceful English furnishings, intimacy, and fine food. It was also a perfect example of what she would be giving up if she left New Orleans.

Over a delicious dinner of shrimp bisque followed by marinated filet mignon, they confined their talk to idle things. They discovered a mutual love for mystery novels that began on a dark and stormy night, walks on a beach at sunset, the taste of chocolate, and the smell of freshly cut grass. He teased her about being a doom-and-gloom movie aficionado and defended his preference for witty comedies. She admitted to being a junk food junkie. He confessed his addiction to running.

After the meal, Drew leaned back in his chair, feeling replete from the excellent food and perfectly content with his companion. He watched her sip the last of her wine and took delight in the way the candlelight brought out the red-gold in her wild cloud of hair.

She was lovely, he thought. Her teal crepe dress draped Grecian style from one shoulder, then fell in graceful folds around her slender body, clinging in all the right places. Its deep color gave her skin a translucent glow.

Catching him staring, she smiled at him over the rim of her crystal goblet. As always, her killer smile took his breath away and the word *forever* popped into his mind.

"Enjoying?" he asked.

"Of course. Who wouldn't enjoy the luxury of being served by their own maid and butler for the evening?"

He smiled. "New Orleans does have the best of everything. Food. Music. Culture. Anything is possible here."

"Everything is lovely." Her gaze swept the room, then returned to him. "And so are you."

His laughter was deep and full-hearted. "That's supposed to be my line. *You* are lovely. I'm just pleasantly attired."

Amen to that, Caitlin thought. His evening clothes had been tailor-made in the 1920s. Yet the dinner jacket, pleated white shirt, black silk cummerbund, and black trousers with braid on the seams looked as though they'd been cut and sewn especially for him. He wore the attire with unconscious casual elegance.

The butler appeared at Drew's side. As the two men held a discussion about after-dinner coffees, Caitlin took the chance to study Drew across the candlelit table. Little things about him were becoming endearing to her. Like the way he tilted his head when listening to someone, and his always-ready smile.

She marveled over his ability to approach every experience as though it were new and exciting. His strength of character was admirable. Instead of imploding into a million dust particles under the weight of a lifetime of loneliness and neglect, he'd become a diamond.

She knew he cared for her. A man like Drew didn't go to the lengths he did to attract a woman's attention unless his emotions were involved.

As if sensing her scrutiny, he looked at her and smiled. His eyes communicated the expression she knew her own reflected. The essence of desire was so strong, she felt as if it could actually spill out onto the table.

With frightening clarity, she knew she could easily grow used to a lifetime of seeing him seated across the table from her. An equilibrium-shaking tremor swept through her body.

No! The single word echoed in her mind. Becoming dependent on Drew wasn't a part of her plan. It could dull her judgment, force her to make decisions she didn't want to make.

She hid her confusion by turning her attention to the black-lacquered Chinese screen that preserved their alcove's privacy.

Drew murmured something to the butler, and the other man moved away. Then Drew reached out and laced his fingers with hers.

All too conscious of the perfect fit of their entwined hands, Caitlin felt a tingle of apprehension. Fear, she realized, was much like joy—all consuming. She rebelled against it. Tonight, she simply wanted to enjoy the moment.

"Are your parents shocked by the fact that you share a house with a man?" he asked.

She looked at him curiously, wondering where that question had come from. "Not at all. They trust my judgment." Humor sparkled in her eyes. "My dad sees the city, any big city, as a dangerous animal ready to gobble up lone females."

Drew grinned. "He isn't worried about me gobbling you up?"

Her dad should be more worried about her gobbling him up, she thought. She laughed, still amazed at how easily laughter came to her when she was with him. "No. He thinks you'll protect me. My mom is thrilled. She has high hopes that you're the Prince Charming she's been wishing for."

"Pushing for marriage is she?" he teased.

"Oh, yes. I keep telling her I'll probably never find the kind of man who is willing to put up with the demands of my career. But she believes somewhere there's a man with my name on him."

Yeah, Drew thought. *Me.*

"Don't misunderstand," she went on. "I love my mother. We're very close. We just disagree on that particular subject." She frowned. "And you know, that's always puzzled me. She knows how difficult it is to make sacrifices for someone else. She gave up her career to marry my father."

A warning signal went off in Drew's mind. "Why didn't she keep performing after she married? Your father doesn't sound like the kind of man who would object to his wife working if she wanted to."

"He isn't. I think he was very proud of her success.

She was beginning to get starring roles just before she quit. They were living in Atlanta then, and I told you how my dad dislikes cities. Mom was offered a position with a touring company. After her first tour, she decided she couldn't stand being away from Dad for months at a time. She also knew he was unhappy with his job and that he hated living in the city. So she quit, and they moved back to Dahlonega where my dad grew up."

The butler returned with café au lait. When he left them again, Caitlin picked up the delicate demitasse and stared thoughtfully into the steaming liquid. "I never want to put myself in the position of having to make that kind of decision."

Drew studied her deceptively composed features. Was her last statement a veiled warning for him not to get too close to her? Choosing a humorous approach to put his suspicions to the test, he said, "So, I guess that means I should cancel the wedding invitations and tell the minister we won't be living happily ever after in New Orleans, huh?"

Caitlin gazed intently at him for a moment. The featherlike laugh lines around his eyes told her he was joking. She relaxed and teased him back. "That would be a wise move. Unless, of course, you're willing to follow me to Baltimore, Houston, Chicago, or Los Angeles."

"I'd much rather convince you to stay here." He smiled persuasively. "All things considered, it wouldn't be a bad deal. You'd get me, a beautiful home, and a great partnership in a multidisciplinary practice." He paused to gesture casually at their surroundings. "And, of course, the best restaurants."

Caitlin lowered her eyes. She had a feeling he wasn't kidding anymore. An invisible tremor raced beneath her skin.

She lifted her chin, meeting his steady gaze with

cool reserve. "As tempting as that offer may be, I'm not going into private practice. And although I do enjoy the occasional elegance of an evening like this, I'm just as happy with a taco and diet cola."

Drew felt tension engulf them like a heavy mist. He knew he'd gone too far, and she'd seen through his verbal slight of hand. He started to speak, hoping to smooth things over, but she spoke first.

"Suppose we were to fall in love," she said, her voice unusually sharp. "Suppose I was offered the research/study position in Houston. What would you say if I asked you to relocate with me?"

His face clouded with chagrin. He didn't like being put on the defensive, but the undisguised challenge in her eyes nailed him. He knew an outright refusal could damage their fragile relationship. Yet the thought of being uprooted from his home was inconceivable.

Again, he took refuge in humor. "Shrimp bait, why would you want to trade a subtropical paradise for a desert full of tumbleweeds? People talk funny there and put on ten-gallon hats to go out cow poking on weekends. I've heard they grow rattlesnakes the size of boa constrictors. Imagine walking up and finding one of those creatures in bed with you."

Regret filled Caitlin. She carefully schooled her expression to remain calm, yet she couldn't keep a slight chill from invading her voice. "What makes this city so special?"

His eyes darkened with emotion. "It gives me a sense of belonging," he said quietly. "I've been shuffled around from place to place since I was six. Until I put down roots here in New Orleans, I never allowed myself to think in terms of anything permanent. Now I have a home that belongs to me, and I want to fill it with people who belong with me. I intend to raise a family and grow old in this place. I don't want to start over again."

Vividly, she recalled the things he'd told her about the loneliness and uncertainty of his childhood. Somewhere along the way, the idea of staying in one place had come to mean home and acceptance to him. She clearly understood his great need for some-place and someone to call his own. His house and the city had become his security blanket, she thought sadly. One he would fight to keep.

Yet as much as she understood, she couldn't stop herself from saying, "You're pinning an awful lot of hopes and dreams on a piece of real estate and a spot on the map."

The magic of the evening suddenly departed for Drew, leaving a bitter taste in his mouth like stale, cheap champagne. "It may sound too simplistic to you, but everyone needs a place to call home. And this is mine."

Knowing the discussion would disintegrate into an argument if they continued, he took her hand again and tried to rekindle the magic. "If you're finished, I thought we might go up to the Rainforest for a while."

Caitlin was silent. A private war raged inside her mind. Her emotional system was overloading. She found she couldn't resist staying with him for just a little while longer. Tomorrow would be soon enough to work on her resolve to keep her heart and her future plans intact.

She smiled, though she was sure there was a hint of melancholy to it. "Yes. I'd like that. I've never been there before."

Drew paid the check, and they walked out to the lobby.

"Does it actually rain up there?" she asked as he led her to the elevator.

"Oh, yes." He tucked her hand in the crook of his arm. "The light show is fantastic. You feel like you're in the middle of an island storm. The dance floor surrounds a tropical rain forest. The view of the city and the river is stunning at night. I think you'll like it."

When they stepped off the elevator and into the bar, the pounding beat of a popular rock group was just ending. Caitlin stood transfixed as the rain forest came alive.

The hint of a gentle breeze softly rustled through the vegetation. Thunder cracked overhead and the downpour commenced. She closed her eyes, listening to the rhythmic sound of falling rain. She could almost feel the wind and moisture on her face and smell the fresh scent of tropical flowers.

Arms slid around her and locked at her waist. "It's so real, isn't it?" Drew whispered in her ear. "You can almost believe you're actually on a South Seas island."

She leaned back against him, imagining the two of them alone in such a paradise. It spawned a few new fantasies that would have made her blush if spoken aloud.

Slowly the shower subsided. There was a momentary hush, then soft music, lovers' music, filled the silence.

"Would you like to dance?"

Still spellbound, she murmured agreement.

They walked onto the crowded dance floor. She went into his arms as if she'd done so a thousand times before. Resting her face against his chest, she gave herself up to the honeyed melody. As she listened to the sound of his heartbeat, everything around her became a blur of swirling colors and motion. She pressed closer, feeling a state of exquisite sensual awareness heighten her senses. Moving as if lost in a dreamworld, she swayed in harmony with the music. It was a night of pure fantasy, she thought. One she knew would long remain in her heart's memory.

Drew felt alive with currents of sexual longing. Blinding flames of need made him raw with wanting. He ran his hands down her back, fingertips meeting at the base of her spine. Drawing her deeper into the cradle of his body, he bent his head to kiss her hair, breathing in the subtle fragrance of her perfume.

As the music faded, she raised her head and found him looking at her with undisguised longing touched with a hint of sadness.

No matter what their bodies wanted from each other, she realized now, that more than ever, the odds were against them. Only heartbreak could come of anything between them.

Seven

The next morning, Caitlin woke up grumpy and tired from tossing and turning all night. She lay in bed, listening to Drew belt out a song. It was "What Kind of Fool Am I." She could gladly give him a detailed description on that subject. Her gaze drifted to the clock on the table beside her bed. It was only eight.

Groaning, she dragged herself out of bed, threw on her favorite crinkled cotton robe, then stumbled toward the kitchen.

Drew stopped singing when he saw Caitlin standing in the doorway. With her arms folded across her waist and a cross expression on her face, he knew she was not a happy woman this morning. Smiling brightly, he poured freshly brewed coffee into a Garfield mug.

"Good morning." He walked over to her and handed her the mug.

Wrapping both hands around the grinning cartoon cat, she drifted over to the glass-top table and fell into a chair. She took a sip, then stared at him.

He leaned against the pantry cabinet and watched her assess him from the feet up.

Even though it was disgustingly early, Caitlin could appreciate his long, sinewy legs. They weren't overly hairy, which was good. She wasn't fond of hairy men. Her gaze drifted upward past the shorts that emphasized the slimness of his hips, traveled on to the Tulane T-shirt stretched across his broad chest, then rested on his face.

"Have I mentioned," she began with ominous calm, "that I hate getting up early on my day off? And I might add, I'm not too fond of cheerful people first thing in the morning either."

Her eyes narrowed as his only response was a broad grin. "Why are you smiling at me like that?"

"Because." Drew pushed away from the cabinet and walked toward her. "I . . ." His words got lost in an avalanche of feeling that caught him completely off guard. Stopping in front of her, he raised his hand to touch her cheek.

"What?" she whispered. Unable to resist, she turned her head slightly to press her lips to his palm.

He finger combed her sleep-tangled hair back from her face. What would she do, he mused, if he mentioned the word love? Withdraw into one of her distant stares? Get up and back out of the room, murmuring something about having bags to pack?

Keep it light, he advised himself. He tickled her cheek, then dropped his hand back to his side. "Because I like you in the morning even though you're such a grump."

"Nobody likes me in the morning. Not even my family." She downed the coffee, then lifted the mug in supplication. "Please, sir, more coffee."

He obligingly took the cup and walked back across the kitchen to refill it. Returning to her, he said, "It's yours on one condition."

Caitlin didn't like his have-I-got-a-deal-for-you tone. She slumped down in the chair and propped her chin in her palm. "It's not wise to withhold a caffeine addict's coffee."

"Go for a run with me, and I'll supply your addiction for a year."

"You've got to be kidding."

He shook his head. "No run. No coffee."

"I hate you."

"That's the caffeine monkey on your back talking." He picked up the glass coffeepot and held it over the sink. "Maybe I should do you a favor and just dump the whole potful down the drain. You'll thank me for it someday."

"Oh, all right." She eyes him stonily. "I'll run with you." She got up and took the full mug from him. On her way out of the kitchen, she opened a cabinet and grabbed a chocolate snack cake. If she was going to run, she needed a quick energy fix.

"That's not good for you," Drew called after her.

"Tough," she shouted back, tearing open the cellophane wrapper.

A short while later, she returned, her face freshly scrubbed, her hair pulled back in a ponytail, and dressed in a pair of gray sweatpants and a T-shirt. "Okay, let's get this over with. Hit the street, buster."

Drew tossed the sports section of the Saturday paper onto the table. Grinning, he got up and followed her to the door.

"Something tells me you aren't into exercise," he said.

"I can't imagine how you came to that conclusion."

He laughed and held the door open for her.

Two hours later, Caitlin practically fell into the kitchen as she stumbled through the door. She was hot, tired, sweaty, out of breath, and close to dying. Muscles she'd never had any trouble with before protested each step as she limped to the sink. Groaning, she turned on the faucet and splashed cold water on her face.

"Now, that wasn't bad, was it?" Drew asked from behind her.

Leaning over the sink, she turned her head to give him a killing look. She'd huffed and puffed all the way to Audubon Park and back. He was barely winded.

"You did pretty well for your first run," he said, taking a glass out of a cabinet.

Last run, she corrected silently.

He filled the glass with water and drained it, then he playfully smacked her rear. "Running gets into your blood. Just wait and see. You're going to love it."

She resisted the urge to wrap her hands around his throat. "Get real, Daniels. I'm a couch potato. I'm a junk food junkie, a caffeine addict, and I'm morally opposed to all forms of torture, including exercise."

Laughing, Drew just shook his head. He'd thoroughly enjoyed having her run with him, even though she'd slowed him down and complained all the way. If nothing else, he knew it had helped to relieve the sexual tension threatening to override his good intentions.

The phone rang. "I'll get it," he said. Setting his glass on the counter, he headed for the telephone mounted on the wall beside the refrigerator.

"Hello?" He listened to the soft, musical voice on the other end for a second, then said, "Yes, she is. Just a moment."

He muffled the receiver against his chest and looked across the kitchen. Caitlin was still hunched over the sink. She'd commandeered his glass and was gulping down water. "Catie, dear, your mother wants to speak to you."

She rushed over to take the phone. "Mom! How are you? . . . Yes, I miss you too."

"Was that Dr. Daniels who answered?" Ellen MacKenzie asked.

"Yes, it was." Caitlin ignored her mother's tell-me-more tone. "Have you seen Stephen lately?"

"Yes, he came home last weekend and brought his new girlfriend. Her name is Jenny. Pretty little thing. An art major, I believe. Stephen seems crazy about her. I wouldn't mind having her for a daughter-in-law."

Caitlin scowled at Drew, who was tickling her neck. "I wouldn't start planning the wedding yet, Mom. You know Stephen falls in love twice a week."

She tried to move away from the fingers tracing her spine, but found herself caught around the waist and pulled into the cradle of Drew's thighs. "I'm sorry, what did you say, Mom?"

"I said your Dr. Daniels sounds very nice."

"He's not—oh, good grief." She jerked her neck away from Drew's gesturing lips. "Hold on just a second, Mom."

She put her palm over the receiver. "Would you stop that!" she hissed at him. "I'm talking to my mother, for pity's sake."

"Let me talk to her," he said, grabbing for the phone.

"No!" She slapped at his hand.

"Tell her I want to speak to her."

"Hush." She put the receiver back to her ear. "Oh, no, not you, Mom. It's just Drew. He says to tell you hello. . . . What? I . . . All right." She held the phone out to him. "She wants to talk to you."

"Hello, Mrs. MacKenzie," he said eagerly, and let go of Caitlin. "Yes, that's right, I'm a pediatrician. Right, this is my last year of residency too. I'm looking forward to opening my own practice in New Orleans. In fact, I've been trying to convince your daughter to go into practice with me. . . . No, no luck so far. . . . You do that. . . . Well, it's a pleasure to finally speak to you too. Catie talks about you often."

He raised a skeptical brow at Caitlin. "She's told you all about me? Then you must think I'm a cross between Genghis Khan and Daffy Duck." He laughed. "Nice things? Do tell. . . . She said that?"

Caitlin watched Drew give her mother his undivided attention. He stretched the phone cord over to the kitchen table where he dropped into a chair. He crossed one sexy ankle over the opposite knee, apparently getting comfortable for a long, cozy chat.

Emitting a low groan, she gently banged her forehead on the refrigerator door. From Drew's end of the conversation, she realized he and her mother were quickly becoming soul mates. Oh, Lord. She murmured a sympathetic prayer for the mailman who would probably end up with a hernia from all the fluff gifts her mother would send.

"Do you know she has the worst eating habits?" she heard Drew exclaim. "I mean, frozen entrées have their place, but not as a steady diet. And she eats Little Debbie snack cakes for breakfast . . . Oh, I'm sure you didn't let her do that at home . . . Yes, I'll make certain she eats properly. You're not to worry. I'll take good care of her for you."

Caitlin glared at him. "I can take care of myself, Daniels," she said, catching his attention. She made strangling motions with her hands.

He just smiled at her, winked, and continued talking to her mother. "Why, thank you . . . Yes, nice talking to you. I hope to meet you and Mr. MacKenzie someday too."

Meeting? Caitlin's eyes widened. They were talking about meeting? She rushed over and snatched the phone from him. "Mom—"

"Drew is a love, Caitlin. I like him already."

"He is? You do?" Oh, dear.

"I'm so glad you aren't alone anymore. You know how your dad worries about you living in the city."

Thoroughly exasperated, she sighed heavily. "Mom, I lived alone for years and never had any trouble."

"Read the papers, darling. Women who live alone are attacked all the time. We feel it's much safer for you to have a roommate."

That's what you think. Caitlin pushed Drew's caressing hand away from her thigh, then bopped him on the head with her fist.

Her father got on the extension, and she spoke with both her parents for a few more minutes, then said good-bye. As she walked across the room to a hang up the phone, she leveled an irritated look at Drew, who was still seated at the table.

"You are the most aggravating man I've ever met," she said. "Where do you get off telling my mother you'll take care of me? I don't need anybody to take care of me or see that I eat properly. If I want chocolate cake for breakfast, that's my decision and none of your business."

"I know you're quite capable of taking care of yourself," Drew said mildly. "But sometimes we all need someone to lean on. That's what friendship is all about. And if it makes your mother happy to believe someone is looking out for you, what's the harm?"

He stood up and walked over to her. "You don't know how fortunate you are that your parents worry about you. I think I'm a bit envious. But I apologize if you think I was out of line."

He was silent for a moment, trying to read her thoughts by studying her unwavering gaze. Coming up blank, he said awkwardly, "I really enjoyed talking to your mother."

He looked at her so apprehensively, Caitlin's heart melted a little. He didn't have an affectionate family.

She supposed it wouldn't hurt to share hers with him on the phone every once in a while.

"I don't mind you talking to my mom," she said. "Just try not to go overboard on this looking after me business when you do speak to her. And for heaven's sake, don't tell her you're trying to convince me to go into practice with you. You know that's impossible."

Nothing was impossible, Drew thought. He only hoped he had enough time to make her understand that.

He smiled brightly. "What do you say we get cleaned up and go out to lunch?"

She sighed, knowing she really shouldn't spend any more time with him than necessary. But somehow, she simply couldn't refuse. "I'll go on one condition."

He tilted his head and stared at her warily. "And that is?"

"Never, *never* make me run again."

He laughed and crossed his heart with one finger. "I promise." Sliding his arm around her shoulders, he started walking her out of the kitchen. "I know this great little health food place on—"

"NO! No health food."

"Aw, Catie, you'll love it."

"Hamburgers," she insisted. "I want a fat, juicy hamburger. With tons of greasy french fries."

They hadn't gone more than a few steps when the phone rang again.

"I'll get it," Drew said. He turned back to the kitchen.

While he was talking, Caitlin wandered out to the foyer to see if the mail had come. A pile of letters and bills lay scattered on the floor below the mail slot in the door. She picked them up and began sorting them into his, hers, and theirs. The address on one of the envelopes caught her attention. It was from the research facility in Chicago. She dropped everything else onto a table.

For a moment, she simply stared at the address. Fear and excitement mingled within her. Her whole future could be contained inside the business-size white envelope. Her heart pounded. Her throat went dry. With trembling fingers, she tore it open, withdrew the single sheet of stationery, and eagerly scanned the letter.

"Catie, where are—Oh, there you are." Drew walked over to her. "I'm afraid I'll have to give you a rain check on lunch. Maybe we can go out to dinner tonight instead. I have to go in to work for a while."

Drew suddenly realized she wasn't listening. He took in the flat expression in her eyes and the letter in her hand. "Bad news?"

Swallowing a large lump of disappointment, she folded the sheet of paper and stuffed it back into the envelope. "I just got a thanks-but-no-thanks letter from the research program in Chicago."

"Oh." It was all he could say. Expressing appropriate sympathy was impossible when joy was bubbling up inside him. He knew he was a jerk to feel so happy over her rejection, but he couldn't help it.

However, he felt he should say something to lighten the blow. "It's probably just as well. You wouldn't like the Windy City." He gave her a teasing smile. "It's too cold up there for a Southern girl like you."

"I'm not in the mood for jokes," she said curtly. "This is too important to me."

"Sorry. I was just trying to make you feel better."

"Well, you're not, so cut it out." She stuck the letter into the waistband of her sweatpants, then sagged against the foyer table. Crossing her arms over her chest, she stared down at the floor.

After a moment it registered with her that Drew

was going back to work. Frowning, she looked up at him. "Why are you going in today?"

Glad to change the subject, Drew said, "A patient of mine, Joey Anderson, has started his protocol of treatment for lymphatic leukemia. For some reason, his white cell count dropped this morning. I need to find out what's going on."

"Can't the resident on duty handle that?"

He shrugged. "Well, yes, but Joey's different. The kid's got a special magic and a pair of sapphire-blue eyes that really get to me. I left word to be notified immediately of any change in his condition."

Caitlin unwound the elastic band holding her ponytail while she digested what he'd said. It sounded to her as if he was more intrigued with the child than the case itself. That wasn't good. Getting personally involved with a patient meant potential heartbreak at best, and at worst it meant losing professional objectivity.

"Do you mean you're getting emotionally attached to the child?" she asked pointedly. "Isn't that a bit risky?"

To her surprise he bristled. "No, I'm not. Jeez, Catie, he's only five years old. He's sick and alone. His mother is a widow with five more kids at home. She works two jobs to support the family, so she can't be with him very often. I think even you can understand the child needs to see a familiar friendly face every once in a while."

"Why does it have to be yours?" She gave him an indignant look. "And just what are you implying when you say even *I* can understand that?"

"Figure that one out for yourself," he snapped. "You're the one who's going into research to get away from dealing with patients on a personal level."

Caitlin stiffened. "That's a lousy thing to say. My reasons for wanting to do research have nothing to do with how I feel about dealing one-on-one with patients."

Rocking back on his heels, he ran his fingers through his hair. "Look, I don't want to fight with you. And I think you're just taking your disappointment out on me."

Several seconds of tense silence passed as they stared at each other.

Finally, Drew shook his head. "I have to get dressed." He turned and left her glaring after him.

The following Monday morning, Caitlin sat at the chart desk in the ob/gyn nurses' station. She was supposed to be updating patient information, but she just stared moodily at the chart in front of her.

She'd gotten over her disappointment at being turned down by the Chicago facility. She refused to think negatively because of one rejection. Baltimore, Houston, and Los Angeles had yet to respond. The Human Development and Research Institute in Houston was the one she really had her heart set on anyway.

Tapping a pen against the chart, she realized Drew was the real reason she was feeling so down. He was driving her crazy. He got to her in a way that no man ever had before. But their needs and ambitions were poles apart.

The disagreement they'd had on Saturday had put a bit of a damper on the rest of the weekend. And his dig about her reasons for not becoming a practitioner had given her a few bad moments. Fortunately, after carefully thinking it through, she knew in her heart there was no validity in what he'd said.

A sudden burst of laughter, catcalls, and applause interrupted her thoughts. She turned to look behind her, then nearly fell off her chair.

Craig Paulsen was doing an impression of a fla-
menco dancer for the other interns, residents, and
students waiting for grand rounds. Between his
pearly whites was a long-stemmed red rose. A white
envelope attached to the stem kept hitting him on
the chin.

She was just as amazed as the rest of the ob/gyn
staff by the change in the intern's personality. Everyone thought she was responsible for his miraculous
turnaround, but she knew she really owed Drew for
giving her a hint on how to handle the situation.
Since her talk with him, the intern had become
increasingly cooperative and pleasant.

Craig's flashing blue eyes suddenly lit upon Caitlin. "Look what just came for you, Dr. MacKenzie." He
danced toward her. "Olé!" he shouted, and tossed the
rose into her lap.

She sat perfectly still for a moment as a dozen pairs
of eyes stared at her. Their blatant curiosity made
her feel very uncomfortable.

"Okay, you bums, you've had your fun," Debbie
Wilson said. "The Director of Obstetrics will be here
any minute, and he will not be a happy camper if he
finds you all acting like a bunch of idiots."

Everyone instantly found some way to look busy.

Caitlin mouthed thank you to Debbie for rescuing
her.

Turning her back to the group, she picked up the
rose and stroked its velvety petals. Her pulse beating
an erratic tattoo, she removed the card from the
attached envelope.

Eight

A smiley-face heart was drawn on the enclosed card along with a message that read: *I'm sorry we quarreled on Saturday.* No signature, but she knew it was from Drew.

On one hand, she was charmed and delighted. She could feel a goofy grin just dying to take over her face. On the other hand, she couldn't help feeling a little miffed over Drew's lack of discretion.

The entire Riverview staff loved gossip. Caitlin had always been careful not to give the tattle-mongers any reason to talk about her. At her first opportunity, she'd thank Drew for his romantic gesture and ask him to refrain from doing that sort of thing at work.

Masked and gowned, Drew walked through the Intensive Care Nursery. He stopped by an Isolette to visit with a premature infant girl. Amanda had been with them for several weeks and seemed to be past the critical stage.

"Morning, Manda Panda," he said. "I see you've gained two ounces. What a good girl you are."

Amanda's wizened face crinkled as though she were responding to his praise. She yawned. Sleepy eyes blinked at him, then closed.

Drew reached his hand into the Isolette's opening to pat the baby's back. "Sweet dreams, angel."

"I wish you'd get yourself a woman and have a houseful of babies. Then you might leave mine alone."

Drew turned his head to smile at the head nurse. A grandmotherly woman in her early fifties and built along feather-pillow proportions, Betty was the undisputed matriarch of the Intensive Care Nursery.

"You're always spoiling my babies," she complained, though her pale blue eyes twinkled at him.

"Fish spoil, Betty my love, not babies."

"Humph! Quit worrying that child and get your butt outta my nursery, boy."

"Aye, aye, Captain." He delivered a crisp salute, then turned to leave.

"That new nurse on second shift is a nice girl," Betty said. "You ought to ask her out."

Usually, Drew responded to Betty's matchmaking with a proposal of marriage or a bawdy proposition. But not today. He stood with his hand on the doorknob for a full beat and missed his cue. Smiling, he looked back at the gray-haired woman. "I already have a nice girl." He winked at the surprised nurse and left her to the small charges.

A mental vision of Caitlin accompanied him into the antechamber. His heart rate kicked into overdrive, and he was grinning as he stripped off his mask and gown.

He knew she was beginning to care for him. She just had too much iron will and determination to accept it yet. From now until July, he wasn't about to let her forget him for a minute. One way or the other, he'd show her how good he could make life for the two of them right there in the place where they both belonged.

Caitlin's day went steadily downhill. When she came back from morning rounds, another gift was waiting for her. It was a mechanical toy clown that did back flips when wound up. The card accompanying it read: *I flip over you.*

Just before lunch, she received a heart-shaped red balloon with a card reading: *You have my heart on a string.*

She took the balloon into Debbie's office. "This has got to stop. That man is driving me crazy again."

Debbie looked up from her desk. "Another present from Dr. Daniels? That man's got it bad. I should be so lucky."

"I wish it was you," Caitlin said, tying the balloon to a wire basket sitting on top of a filing cabinet. "Then everybody would be talking about you instead of me."

She flopped down in a chair. "I hate being the subject of gossip."

"I think you're worried about nothing."

Caitlin absently reached for a piece of paper lying on the desk and curled its edges. "Oh, yeah? Even some of my patients are teasing me about my secret admirer."

Debbie moved the paper out of her reach. "That's next week's schedule you're destroying. I've spent days juggling picky folks around, and I won't have you shredding my hard work."

Rising, Debbie tacked the nursing schedule on a bulletin board right next to pictures of Dennis Quaid and James Earl Jones.

"Just don't make a big deal out of it," she said, sitting again. "The talk will die down."

Caitlin sighed. "Did you know they've started placing bets on the identity of my secret admirer?" She'd told only Debbie who was sending the gifts. But she didn't think it would be long before someone made the connection between her and Drew. Then she was doomed. At Riverview, the only subject more interesting than one's own love life was somebody else's.

"I heard about the bets," Debbie said.

Caitlin could see she was trying not to laugh. "It isn't amusing."

"I think you two are perfect for each other. When did you start dating him? Are you as nuts about him as he seems to be about you?"

"About two weeks ago. And I like him a lot. We're sort of semiplatonic friends right now. He knows I'm leaving New Orleans in July, so we're a little hesitant about getting too involved."

The grin Debbie had been holding back suddenly materialized. "You may be hesitant, but I don't think he is."

Before Caitlin could reply to that, someone knocked on the office door. It opened just wide enough for Craig Paulsen to stick his head inside the room. His wide grin told her he'd heard about her latest gift.

"So, Dr. MacKenzie," he said jovially. "How's your love life?"

She gazed coolly at him. "If you don't have a job to do, Dr. Paulsen, I'll be happy to give you an assignment. How do you feel about bedpans?"

The intern held up one hand in surrender. "Say no more. I'm gone. Ciao, baby." He closed the door quickly.

"Ciao, baby?" she repeated in astonishment.

Debbie cracked up laughing.

Caitlin gave her a pained look. "May I use your phone? I think I better call Drew."

"Help yourself. I'll see you later."

Debbie left the office, and Caitlin dialed the pediatric unit. Drew wasn't available so she gave the nurse's aide who answered the call a message for him.

Drew was in the sun room where he was spending his brief lunch break with a group of four-to-six-year-old patients.

"Dr. Daniels," a woman said, walking into the room. "I have a phone message for you."

He looked up and smiled at the aide. "Thanks, Denise," he said, accepting the folded piece of paper.

"The woman who called wouldn't leave her name. Said you'd know who she is."

Caitlin immediately came to his mind. No doubt she couldn't wait to thank him. In his enthusiasm to unfold the note, he missed the odd look the young woman gave him before walking away.

He read the message. It knocked the smile right off his face. He read it again. *Stop it immediately or you're a dead man. Your lack of discretion is causing a great deal of gossip and I don't like it.*

For a moment he was genuinely puzzled. All women liked flowers and gifts. But then again, Caitlin MacKenzie wasn't all women. She was different. And she was seriously mad. Had the gifts embarrassed her? Obviously, she didn't enjoy being the center of attention.

Oh, Lord! he thought. He stood up so fast, he tipped over the kid-size chair he'd been sitting in.

"Where you going?" called out a big-eyed little girl everyone called Zoo.

"To make a phone call!" He dashed out of the room and down the corridor.

Minutes later, Drew was on the phone in his cubbyhole office. "What do you mean you can't get in touch with your messenger?" he yelled at the other person on the line. "This is an emergency. Doesn't he have to check in with you? . . . All right. Please try."

He broke the connection. Slumping down in his chair, he muttered, "I'm a dead man." Now what? he wondered.

Maybe he better warn Catie. He dialed the ob/gyn unit. He was told Dr. MacKenzie was in the delivery room. Knowing she was friends with the supervisory R.N., he asked to speak with Debbie.

"Ms. Wilson, this is Dr. Daniels. I need to talk to Caitlin as soon as she's free. It's very important. . . . What? . . . That's nice of you to say, but I rather doubt she thinks we make a cute couple. Thanks. I appreciate your help."

The door to Drew's office opened as he hung up and Mark Gordon walked in. A huge grin dominated his freckled face. "What's up, chief? I heard you got a weird message, then almost ran down three kids and an old lady to get to your office."

Drew frowned. No wonder Catie was upset. You couldn't sneeze in this place and keep it a secret.

"It's after six," Debbie complained, drumming her peach-colored nails on the table. "Michael said he'd meet me for dinner at five-thirty. I'm giving him ten more minutes, then I'm blowing this pop stand with or without him."

Caitlin smiled at her friend. While she waited for the resident she was currently dating, Debbie was keeping her company in the on-call lounge.

"Want me to go find him for you?" Craig Paulsen asked.

Debbie shook her head, and he went back to playing trash can basketball.

"Did you ever connect with you-know-who?" Debbie whispered.

"No," Caitlin said. "But he stopped sending gifts, so I guess he got my message."

Debbie sighed, then turned to face Craig. "I've got a great joke for you," she said.

Caitlin only half-listened as the two began a one-upmanship of raunchy jokes. Her mind was on Drew. She didn't know what to do about the situation between them. Day by day, she cared just a little more about him. But she firmly believed it was only a matter of time before she received a positive response from one of her applications. That weighed heavily on her mind. If she didn't keep a tight rein on her emotions, she was in for a huge dose of heartbreak come July.

Suddenly, Caitlin noticed her companions were silent. She glanced at them. They were staring at something behind her. Debbie's mouth was open, and Craig's lighter burned inches away from the cigarette dangling between his lips.

She twisted around to see what held their attention. Breath left her body like she'd just been kicked in the stomach.

Standing not two feet away was a man who could pass for Richard Gere's younger brother. A black tuxedo hugged his beautifully proportioned body. A top hat rested upon his black hair. In one hand he held a ruby rose and in the other a cassette player.

"Which one of you is Dr. MacKenzie?" he asked in a bedroom voice.

Shock raced along Caitlin's nerve endings. She stammered out, "Sh-sh-she's not—" The rest of her denial was swallowed by her companions' chorus of, "That's her!"

Smiling, the hunk sashayed closer and put the cassette player on the table.

Caitlin congratulated herself for not screaming in frustration and diving under the table. It took every ounce of self-control she possessed to stay glued to her chair when he stroked her cheek with the rose, then dropped it into her lap.

He hit the play button on the cassette player. The lounge was filled with the riotous sound of "Celebration" by Kool & the Gang.

Caitlin's palms started to sweat as the man swiveled his hips in a sensual dance of invitation. The black silk fabric molded to his body as he danced to the pounding rhythm. His fingers waltzed up his torso to the slash of scarlet silk at his throat. The tie came away in his hand. He draped it over her shoulder.

"My God!" Craig yelped. "He's taking his clothes off."

"Wow," Debbie murmured breathlessly.

Caitlin winced as the top hat was placed on her head. She wanted to die.

The Richard Gere look-alike shrugged out of the tuxedo jacket and flung it to the floor. He teased a finger under the red cummerbund around his tapered waist.

Completely mortified, Caitlin jumped up and slapped the cassette player's off button. "That's enough. I know you're only doing your job, but I would appreciate it if you'd leave now." She whipped off the top hat and tie, tossing them onto the table.

"Okay by me," the dancer said with a shrug. "I get paid one way or the other." He took an envelope out of his trouser pocket and handed it to her.

Total silence fell upon everyone while the man gathered his things, then left.

Caitlin tore the envelope open and read the card. *Every day is a celebration with you.*

Whirling around, she stared hard at Debbie and

Craig. They both wore silly grins. "If one word leaks out about what happened in this room, I will know who to blame." She paused, letting the menacing tone of her voice sink in. Then she continued, "Deb, Dr. Faucheaux is around here somewhere. Find him and tell him to cover for me until I get back. Remind him he owes me four hours."

As she stormed out, she heard Debbie say in awe, "It's going to take four hours? Holy smoke, is she lucky."

Fired by rage and too impatient to wait for an elevator, Caitlin dashed up the two flights of stairs to the pediatric unit.

She went first to the residents' on-call lounge and dorm. Her arrival interrupted a poker game. Drew wasn't one of the players. A big, sandy-haired resident eyed her speculatively when she asked where Drew could be found. He gave her directions to one of the children's wards.

Determined to rake Drew over the hot coals of hell, she flew down the corridor. When she reached the ward, she flung the door open and glanced around for him. She saw him surrounded by half a dozen children.

Hunched over at the waist, Drew had one giggling boy clinging to his back, and a little girl attached to each leg. More children circled him, shouting encouragement to the others.

"There's only one way to fight off a monster attack," she heard him say. "This situation calls for Mr. Tickle Fingers!" His hands dive-bombed down to tickle the ribs of the closest child.

From the children's squeals, shouts, and giggles, Caitlin realized this was a familiar game. She saw little arms and legs flail and dance away from Drew's nimble fingers.

The sight was like an ice shower drenching her temper. She could feel her heart practically melting down into her shoes. How could she remain angry with a man who spent his rare moments of leisure time, playing with sick kids?

One by one, the children ran to the "monster cave," which she gathered was a safety zone. Finally, Drew stood alone, hands on hips, surveying their grinning faces.

"Who's that?" a little girl asked, pointing to Caitlin.

Everyone turned to look. From the children's startled expressions, Caitlin had the sudden notion she'd just been cast into the role of the Wicked Witch.

Stammering out an apology, she groped for the door behind her.

"No! Please wait," she heard Drew call out as she fled into the corridor.

A moment later, he caught up with her, stopping her flight by grabbing on to her elbow.

"I don't want to talk to you right now," she said. "Let go." She tried to jerk loose.

He held on to her. "We're going to talk," he said, dragging her toward a supply closet. He opened the door and gently pushed her inside, then quickly followed her in.

"It's dark in here," she said as she felt his hands settle on either side of her hips.

"Be still. I'm trying to find the light switch."

"Well, it's not located on my body." She wiggled out of his grasp.

He chuckled softly. "Just checking."

He found the switch plate, and the second the dim light sprang on, Drew abandoned his calm attitude. "Okay, I think you probably came up here to rip my heart out. Go right ahead. I deserve it."

"You embarrassed me." She stepped away from him, backing up against shelves of linen. "People are gossiping about me, and I don't like it. You've placed me in a very difficult situation."

"I didn't mean to. Honestly. I only wanted you to know you're important to me. Every morning I wake up thinking about you. You make me feel like I could conquer the world. Maybe I got a little carried away. I thought about taking out an ad on a billboard to tell the whole city how crazy I am about you."

She was horrified. "A billboard? Please say you're joking."

He shook his head. "I'm not. But I resisted the temptation." He smiled hopefully. "Makes all the other things seem subtle, huh?"

For a second, she was speechless. The depth of his feelings stunned her. The demonstration of them was a bit overenthusiastic, but she didn't doubt the sincerity behind it. "It's nice that you care. I'm flattered. But, Drew, you're about as subtle as a runaway truck."

"I tried to stop the *Bellygram*. I swear it. I called to warn you, but—Ah, hell. Just kill me and get it over with."

She slowly walked toward him. Grabbing his lab jacket lapels, she pulled him down until they were almost nose-to-nose. "I have never been so mortified in my entire life. If you ever do anything like that again, I will annihilate you."

It took him a second to realize her voice contained no anger. He wasn't sure why, but she was forgiving him. "Did you hate it?"

She grimaced and released him. "The *Bellygram* was awful. But everything else was . . . okay. I just wish you hadn't sent them to me at work."

Crossing her arms over her waist, she moved back to the shelves and leaned against them. "Do you have any idea how embarrassing it is to have a stranger do a bump and grind in your face?"

Swallowing a laugh, Drew shook his head. He walked over to her, bracing his hands on the shelf above her head. "I'm sorry." He bent down to kiss her.

At first, she simply stood still and let him kiss her. A small, insistent voice warned her not to participate. She really shouldn't. But something electric was happening inside her.

Her arms slid up his chest to his neck. She threaded her fingers through the silky hair lying against his nape. Her lips parted, and he rushed in hungrily.

Caitlin gave herself up to the feeling of rightness. Doubts and possible problems just disappeared when he kissed her. Air seemed trapped in her lungs; passion and tenderness flowed like honey. When he kissed her, she could forgive him for anything. Sensation after sensation rushed through her. She forgot about everything but the wild, swirling need he aroused in her.

Feeling himself nearing the point of no return, Drew at last broke the contact. He rested his forehead on hers. "Why aren't you ripping my heart out?"

Fighting her way out of a sensual fog, Caitlin gave him a blank look. Then she asked herself the same question. The only answer she came up with was that her feelings for him were simply too powerful to shut off or ignore.

She sighed. "I don't know. Maybe it has something to do with your alter ego."

"My what?" He raised his head to look into her eyes.

"Mr. Tickle Fingers."

He smiled sheepishly. "Oh. That's a little game the kids love," he said almost apologetically.

His gaze wandered over her face, then lowered to the white column of her throat. One more kiss, he told himself. Just one more. He recaptured her lips, giving her a hard, demanding kiss.

Breath departed her lungs as renewed excitement surged through her. She drank in the frenzied hunger flowing between them. Instinctively, she pressed closer to the warmth of his lean, hard body.

Drew felt her ardent response with every nerve he possessed. Body, heart, and soul. That's what he wanted from her.

Groaning into her sweet mouth, he drew back. "I think it's only fair to warn you that I want much more than you're prepared to give."

"Yes, I know," she answered in a tight voice.

When she remained silent for a moment, he didn't know whether to laugh, cry, or shake a response from her.

"I am sorry you had to take a lot of razzing about my gifts," he said, stroking her face. "Does it really bother you if people talk about us?"

She shrugged. "Yes and no. I grew up in a small town where everyone knew everything about one another. Reputation and character are important in that kind of close environment. I learned to keep a low profile in order not to incur gossip."

She smiled ruefully. "I don't mean to sound ungrateful for your gifts. I can take a little razzing, but I'm not wild about it."

He touched her lips with the tips of his fingers. "I understand. But, Catie, I don't think either of us can deny any longer that we do have a relationship."

"No, I can't deny it," she said slowly, even though logic and reason told her she should. "But you must understand I'm still trying to adjust to the idea. I'm simply not at the shouting-it-from-the-rooftops stage. Nor can I forget that I'm leaving in July and you're staying here."

A range of emotions swept across his face. His

arms circled her shoulders, and he pulled her to his chest. He ached to tell her he loved her, and wanted the whole world to know it. Getting her to love him back wasn't going as smoothly as he'd hoped. She was still talking about leaving. He wanted to hold her. Wanted it all. Right now. This minute.

He sighed into her hair. "All right, love, we'll take it one step at a time."

She raised her head and he gazed down into her eyes, seeing the subtle shade of green deepen with passion. It was impossible to think straight when she looked at him like that.

Their mouths merged in a soul-stealing kiss. He wanted to breathe her into his heart and keep her for his own. *Forever.*

Kissing a path to her ear, he whispered, "It's true, you know. Every day I spend with you is a celebration."

Somewhere inside her soul, another barrier crumbled. It was going to be very difficult, she decided, not to allow herself to care too much about this wonderful man.

The remainder of the week passed quickly. To Caitlin's relief, not one hint leaked out about the *Bellygram.* By Tuesday afternoon, no one expressed the slightest interest in her secret admirer. Everyone was too busy speculating on how long it would take a certain two residents to figure out they were dating the same nurse.

True to his word, Drew seemed content to allow her to set the pace of their relationship. They spent a quiet day off together on Wednesday. That evening they went out to dinner with Drew's friend Mark Gordon and his date. Caitlin enjoyed their company and formed an instant friendship with Mark's companion, a tiny Cajun beauty with a steel-trap mind and a wicked sense of humor.

Thursday, Drew was kept busy with last-minute preparations for the Halloween party. He offered to pick up a costume for her, and she agreed. Caitlin took advantage of the time alone to catch up on errands and household chores.

The night of the Halloween party arrived. Feeling like a total idiot in her hastily acquired costume, Caitlin reluctantly followed Drew into the elevator at Riverview Hospital. Tired of being stared at, she was glad they were alone for the ride up to pediatrics.

She stood in the corner opposite Drew, her arms tightly hugging her waist. She hadn't felt so self-conscious since grade school. Then she'd been forced into a pair of green tights and matching leotard for the role of Peter Pan in the second grade spring fling production.

Glaring at him, she said, "I'm not getting out of this elevator."

Drew shook his head slowly. "Oh, Catie. That's what you said about leaving the house, and the car, and the hospital parking lot."

Poor baby, he thought, smiling. She looked cute in her costume. Actually, she was decently covered. Only her inhibitions were showing.

"I mean it this time," she said. "You're not prying me loose from this elevator."

"Okay, but you're going to get awfully tired of going up and down all night long." He ignored her mutinous grumbles and adjusted the silken folds of the black red-lined cape draping from his shoulders to his knees.

When he looked at her again, she was staring straight ahead. He took the chance to survey her lithe body. She was dressed in black tights and a long-sleeved leotard that did dynamite things for her trim figure. It molded to her curves the way he wanted to.

He'd been very restrained the past few days, trying hard not to push her too far, too fast. It was wearing thin, though, and becoming increasingly difficult not to give in to his feelings. Sometimes he felt like he was bleeding love from every pore. Why it wasn't obvious to her, he didn't know.

"Your wings are catawampus," he said offhandedly.

"No kidding, Drac. I can't keep the damn things on straight."

He swallowed a groan as he watched her wiggle in an attempt to get them back into place. Her movements were innocently seductive. If she wiggled her body like that against his, he'd die a happy man.

He sighed and sidled over to her. "As much as I'm enjoying your efforts, I think you need help. No, don't give me that glacial look! It's not my fault you didn't like the harem outfit. I thought you'd look great in it. How was I to know you'd be so picky? Consider yourself lucky the costume shop was still open. *You* chose this one, not me. I can't help it if you don't like being a bat. Now, turn around."

She murmured a rather graphic expletive. Drew's face split into a wide, sharp-toothed vampire grin. "Later, darling. Right now you need some expert assistance with your wings."

Caitlin showed him her back and submitted stiffly to his pulling and tugging. She couldn't believe she was doing this. If she weren't so crazy about Drew, she wouldn't have touched this foolish costume with a pair of forceps. The things people do for love.

She blinked rapidly. *Love?*

Nine

Caitlin's throat went dry. *Like*, she corrected herself. The things people do for like. A reasonable woman didn't suddenly reach the mind-numbing conclusion that she was in love while wearing a ridiculous costume in an elevator!

Every nerve in her body was standing at attention. Her heart pounded louder than the drum section of a high school marching band. Her breasts rose and fell with her quick, shallow breaths. Dear Lord, she was on the verge of hyperventilation.

Slowly, she turned her head to glance over her shoulder at Drew. She *was* in love with Drew Daniels. Oh, no, what was she going to do now?

Drew carefully smoothed the black taffeta covering the wires that formed her wings, then adjusted the narrow straps attaching the wings, enjoying the excuse to caress her shoulders. "There," he said, giving her sweet bottom a pat before stepping back to admire his handiwork. "Perfect." He looked up to find her staring at him in a most peculiar way. She seemed sort of horrified and bemused at the same time. "Is something wrong?"

"No," she said, inching away from him. "Nothing's wrong. Everything's hunky-dory." What a crock, Caitlin thought. Her whole life had just been turned upside down and inside out. What a mess!

Her knees felt shaky. She placed her hand on the wall to steady herself. Lord, she couldn't believe it. She needed some time to think this thing through.

Taking refuge in irritation, she glared at him. "I hate this absurd costume. I'm going to get you for this."

"Promises, promises. Stop complaining. You make an adorable bat. Love the ears." He leaned down to kiss her, but she jerked away, and he kissed air instead of a pointed bat ear.

"Jeez, Catie," he said, frowning at her. "You hold a grudge better than anybody I know. This is supposed to be fun. So straighten up and . . . uh, fly right.

"Ouch!" He rubbed his arm where she'd punched him. Grabbing the edges of his cape, he flung his arms up while hissing through his bared fangs.

Unfortunately, the elevator doors slid open at that moment. Out of the corner of his eye he glimpsed the startled faces of an elderly couple.

Shock kept his arms stretched out in midair. He saw the woman clutch her big handbag securely to her bosom. The two people backed away quickly, saying, "We'll wait for the next one." The doors closed.

Drew scowled at Caitlin, who was doubled up laughing. "See what you made me do? Oh, Lord, that was embarrassing." His arms fell to his sides.

"I didn't make you do anything."

"You hit me."

"True, but you made an ass of yourself without any help from me."

The elevator finally reached the pediatric floor. Drew stepped out and kept the doors from shutting.

"Well, are you going to come or not? I need help with the IV, you know."

"Oh, why not. My dignity is in tatters already. Who am I to come between a vampire and his blood supply? Lead on, Drac."

Feeling as if she were willingly going to her own execution, Caitlin followed him down the corridor.

Music and laughter seeped through the door of the residents' on-call lounge and dorm. She knew it was being used as a dressing room, but it sounded like the staff volunteers were doing a little preparty partying.

They entered and were hailed by several costumed people. Caitlin stared around the crowded room, feeling as if she'd been transported to a Hollywood movie studio.

Cinderella was in a corner being zipped into her ball gown by the Mummy. A six-foot gorilla sat at a table playing cards with Charlie Chaplin, a bandit, and the Tin Man. An assortment of ghosts, ghoulies, space creatures, werewolves, and cartoon characters were in various stages of dress and makeup.

Hearing a high-pitched cackle, Caitlin stood on her tiptoes to peer over the head of a giant pumpkin. She recognized Debbie Wilson, who was dressed up as a green-faced witch. She was dancing with her current beau, Michael, who was in a black-and-yellow bumblebee costume. Debbie glanced her way and waved.

Caitlin smiled and started to return the greeting, but was sidetracked by the sight of Harpo Marx duck-walking over to her. He blasted her with a taxi horn, then thrust his knee into her hand.

"Sorry, pal," Drew told Harpo, alias Mark Gordon. "This bat is taken."

Harpo removed his knee from Caitlin's hand. His synthetic curls shook sadly. "That's the story of my life. Nobody wants to be my bat."

"What happened to Alicia?" Caitlin asked, inquiring about the Cajun beauty she'd liked so much.

"She dumped me," he said mournfully. "Party at the Marriott after this wingdig. Pass the word." He turned and used his taxi horn to clear a path through the crowd.

Placing a proprietary arm around Caitlin's waist, Drew tugged her along in Harpo's wake.

Caitlin relaxed. She no longer felt strange in her formfitting costume. Some others were much worse. She also was glad to see that Drew's possessive hand on her waist elicited nothing more than a few friendly smiles. Thanks to Harpo, half the hospital now knew she and Drew were dating, and no one seemed to care.

She helped attach Drew to an IV pole that held a bag of fake blood. To her amazement, he then took charge of the group and soon had everyone organized and ready to begin the night's festivities. Oddly enough, she realized he was looked upon as a leader. That was something she hadn't expected. She stood with him as he gave last-minute instructions to people as they filed out the door.

When the last one went out, she started to follow. He stopped her by latching on to her wings, then he closed the door.

"Have we forgotten something?" she asked, swinging around to face him.

He smiled provocatively and reached for her hand. "I think so."

The touch of his lips on her palm activated her nerve endings. Her pulse went into overdrive. The temperature-controlled room suddenly seemed overly warm and filled with electric currents.

Drew slid his hands slowly up her arms and pulled her closer. Her body fit perfectly against his. He almost groaned aloud as her fingers slipped beneath his cape and caressed his waist. She raised her face, inviting a kiss.

The last four days had been the longest of his thirty years. Trying to keep his promise not to rush their relationship, he'd hardly dared to touch her for fear of going up in flames.

He curved his hands around her hips, drawing her closer to the heat of his body. Mercy, but she felt good, he thought hazily. *He* felt good just touching her. He could swear the *whole* world felt fine at the moment. Their bodies melded together in a perfect fit. He lowered his head toward her waiting lips.

Caitlin closed her eyes in anticipation. She eagerly sought his mouth.

Their parted lips met and quickly separated.

He muttered an oath.

She rubbed her knuckles across her abused mouth.

He ran his tongue over his plastic fangs.

They stood looking at each other with a mixture of longing and disbelief.

Caitlin started to laugh. "Kissing a vampire is dangerous. No, don't take your fangs out. We should go. The ankle biters are waiting."

She turned toward the door before she could change her mind about wrestling him to the floor and kissing him senseless. Besides, she still needed time to think about this love thing.

Drew gazed after her. As much as he adored kids, he suddenly wished he could send the whole bunch on a hike. A long one. He sighed and followed her out, trailing his portable blood supply.

They headed for the Sun Room where the main events were to take place. Drew spotted four little girls coming out of a ward. "Good e-ven-ing, ladies." He inclined his head, trying to look properly vampir-ish. "This is my friend Igor," he said, pointing to

Caitlin. "Could you show us the way to the blood bank? We want to make a withdrawal."

The girls giggled and scurried away.

"Wrong story, Drac," Caitlin said dryly. "Igor was a hunchback, not a bat."

"Your humps may be in the wrong place, but Igor was always a little batty." His smile deepened into laughter as he watched the expression on her face. She was such a delight to tease, and always fell so nicely for his jokes. He danced away from her fist before it could connect with his jaw.

Caitlin stared after the chuckling vampire as he strolled down the corridor, rolling the IV beside him. She sighed. "I've got to stop being his straight man."

"Come along, Igor, my sweet," he called back, turning to blow her a kiss. "You've got a job to do."

The large, glass-walled Sun Room was chaotic. Caitlin stood at the entrance and took in the scene of excited children, parents, and volunteers. Orange and black crepe paper, gossamer webs, and glowing creatures hung from the ceiling. One side of the room was cordoned off in a makeshift haunted house. Eerie noises, moans, and screams floated out from it. There was a fortune teller's tent, various games set up on the opposite side, and a section of tables and refreshments.

Caitlin spent the next few hours dispensing such delicacies as Witches Brew (apple juice), Eye-of-Newt (grapes), Ghost Slime (lime Jell-O), and Fried Bat Brains (popcorn). She played game master for "Pumpkin, Pumpkin, Who's got the Pumpkin?", then rounded up a group of volunteers to deliver Halloween cheer and trick-or-treat bags to the children who were confined to their rooms.

She and her assistant, Craig Paulsen, were just coming out of a patient's room when they ran into Drew.

"Igor! There you are, you sweet little bat." Drew pinched her cheek in passing.

"I thought Igor was a hunchback," came Craig's puzzled voice from deep within his Yogi Bear suit.

"You're right," Caitlin said, and headed for the next patient on her list.

"Why did he call you Igor?" Craig asked, lumbering after her.

"You're supposed to be smarter than the average bear," she told him. "You figure it out."

After a moment, she heard a low rumble of laughter coming from her partner. It was on the tip of her tongue to tell him he was being un-*bear*-able. She resisted. Drew, she thought wryly, was rubbing off on her in more ways than one. God save her from bad puns and giggling bears.

When she finished delivering treats, she helped tuck excited, wound-up children into bed.

The corridor was nearly deserted when she left the last ward. The silence seemed almost eerie after all the noise and party confusion.

She aimed her tired feet toward the on-call room where she hoped to find Drew. Wondering how she was going to talk him out of joining the volunteer crowd for their party at the Marriott, she didn't hear the sound of a door opening.

A hand snaked out of a supply closet and wrapped around her arm. She squeaked out a scream as she was pulled inside the closet. Another hand clamped over her mouth.

"Hush, it's just me," the familiar voice whispered in the dark.

She nipped at Drew's fingers. His hand was replaced with his mouth. No fangs. He proceeded to kiss her senseless. She responded with reckless abandon.

Caitlin felt herself being lifted. Her soft curves

molded to the lean contours of his body. In the deep mists of intense desire, the world was forgotten. Barriers were lowered. Rules fell by the wayside. Nothing existed but Drew and his intoxicating assault on her senses.

"Uh, Catie?" He ran a string of kisses from her mouth across her cheek.

"Mmmm?"

"I don't . . ." His breath tickled her neck as he kissed her there. "I don't want to party at the Marriott." He slipped his fingers into her hair and breathed in her apple blossom scent.

The velvety murmur of his voice, the intimate darkness, his warmth, his fingers brushing the tips of her breasts mesmerized her. "What party?" She found it impossible to think clearly.

"The staff party."

"Oh," she answered weakly. "No." This time her voice was strong and certain. "I don't want to party at the Marriott. I want to go home with you. I want you. Only you."

Drew walked through his darkened bedroom. There was no hesitancy in his steps. He knew every inch of the room. Could tell the exact spot where his foot might touch a creaking floorboard.

He'd been alone in this house, this room, since the day he'd moved in. Although he'd had several caring friendships with women over the years, he'd been alone emotionally for a very long time. Much too long.

He reached the round cherry table beside his brass bed. His fingers accurately found a small silver box and took out a match. A flame sparked to life. He held it to the wick of a candle. The darkness receded.

Feeling a little nervous, he sat down on the bed to wait for Caitlin.

• • •

The rhythmic pull of the brush through her hair soothed Caitlin's pulsating nerves, and a calm descended upon her. She laid the brush on the vanity table and studied her reflection in the mirror. A little of her mother's serenity showed in her hazel eyes. She appeared to be a woman who knew her own mind. A woman with the knowledge that a man who cared very much for her, one that she loved, waited for her to come to him.

She looked at the door of her bedroom. If she opened that door and went to his room, everything would change. Perhaps after tonight her heart would no longer be completely her own.

Never the kind of person who lived for the here and now, she'd always taken life seriously. Approached decisions carefully. Believed tomorrow depended on how she lived today.

Her future was still hidden behind a nebulous haze. She couldn't quite see through the mist to where her hopes and dreams lay sleeping. Some of these hopes and dreams might take shape, color, tangibility; some might never come true. Whether her future included Drew, she didn't know. It was one of those things just out of reach, hidden from her view.

She took a deep breath, stood up, and left the room. With each step that took her closer to Drew, she felt stronger, more certain this was right. She didn't need more time to understand her feelings. She loved Drew and that was all that mattered.

She entered his bedroom and stopped just beyond the threshold. The room was silent. A single candle flickered yellow flame patterns against the wall, bathing the dark with a warm glow. On the table, beside the candle, was a crystal vase. It held a white rose.

The moment she quietly stepped into the room, Drew's breath suspended. When he saw her close the door behind her, he slowly filled his lungs with air and let it out.

No longer alone. Catie was with him.

He watched her standing very still, her gaze drawn once more to the candle flame. She hadn't noticed him yet. He stood in the shadows.

Never, he thought, had she looked more beautiful. He smiled. Silks and satins couldn't have been more elegant, more endearing, than her familiar cotton robe.

Clasping her arms tightly to her chest, Caitlin searched the darkness for him. Then she saw him. He walked gracefully toward her. One hand crept up to cover her heart. It beat wildly.

She saw that he had also showered and changed. An old pair of jeans rode low on his hips, faithfully outlining his long legs. He'd thrown on a dark shirt, leaving the front unbuttoned. The sleeves were rolled back from his wrists. His feet were bare.

As he came closer, she saw a smoldering green fire in his eyes. His lips formed a teasing, provocative smile as he stopped within arm's length.

"Hello." He said the single word in a deep, husky voice.

She met his gaze. Just one look, she thought as she became lost in his depthless eyes. One look from him could make her tremble. With a faint laugh, she swayed into his outstretched arms. They quickly closed around her. She rested her cheek against the fine sprinkling of sable curls peeking through his open shirt.

A sudden blinding rush of love and need surged straight to her head. She wanted to verbalize the feeling, but it being so new, so fragile, it came out all wrong. "Why do I . . . think I like you so much?"

Drew heard the vulnerability in her voice. He felt it vibrate against his skin. "Because . . ." He paused to place a kiss upon her hair, and his thoughts changed directions. Framing her face with his hands, he tilted her head back to look into her eyes. "Are you certain you want to be with me? I think it's only fair to warn you that I love you."

Her head tipped downward. Her shoulders began to shake.

Drew's heart constricted, the movement at once swift and painful. Tears? Because she didn't want him to love her? Because she didn't care enough for him? A dull ache throbbed at his temple. He felt ill. "What's wrong, Catie?" he asked in a gentle whisper. He was surprised his voice held no hurt or fear.

She raised her head. He breathed a sigh of relief when he saw no trace of tears. Instead humor trembled on her lips.

"You make that sound like a threat," she said. *Drew loved her!* The three simple words were inscribed upon her soul. She smiled enchantingly and reached up to caress his face.

"It's a promise," he murmured. The tenderness in her touch healed the ache. His solemn gaze searched her upturned face. "I need an answer."

She swept a wayward strand of hair from his brow. "There's no one on earth I'd rather be with. I—" Her heart pounded against her breast. "I feel so much for you," she whispered. "I don't quite know what to do with it all."

He drew in a ragged breath. She hadn't said the three words he wanted to hear, but he knew she cared for him. Cared deeply. Gathering her closer, he kissed her, drinking in her fire and passion.

Caitlin slipped her arms over her shoulders. The strength that had carried her across his threshold was deserting her by degrees. Her knees wanted to buckle. Need shivered through her. A barely audible sigh escaped her when their lips parted.

Humming under his breath, Drew began waltzing her in circles to a symphony playing in his mind. They were rhythm and rhyme, he thought, harmony and motion. If she wanted him to, he'd gladly reach up to the heavens and pull down a star for her.

Caitlin felt the backs of her knees touch his bed. She would have fallen if not for the arms holding her safely upright. Staring into his riveting eyes, she seemed to waver in and out of reality. She untied the belt around her waist. The cotton robe fell open.

His hands slid up her body to capture her breasts. Hypnotized by his touch, she felt half spirit, half flesh. She wanted to be closer to him, wrapped in his loving arms.

Her robe slithered past her hips to lie in a pool at her feet along with his shirt. Swirling colors shimmered behind her closed eyelids as magical words and honeyed kisses left a trail of liquid fire along her bare shoulder, down one slender arm, across her midriff.

Sinking to his knees, Drew breathed a sigh against the silk of her stomach. His hands met at the base of her spine. It was eerie, he mused, this feeling of need, passion, and tenderness she brought out in him. She bent over him, sending warm chestnut tresses flowing against his shoulder. He exhaled sharply, tickling the skin beneath his lips. She pressed a kiss to his hair.

Slowly rising, he said her name in a soft litany, communing upward to the velvet undersides of her breasts and on to the hollow of her throat. His mouth met hers in a burning union as he lowered her onto the bed.

Pausing only long enough to prepare himself with the condom he'd placed on the table, he sank onto the bed with her. Seconds later they were tangled together. The weight of Drew's body, his spicy scent, quickened the flow of blood through her veins. She responded to his every touch and he to hers. Quivering beneath his knowing hands, she experienced sensations she'd never fully known before.

Wanting to make him tremble with need for her, too, she pushed him to lie beside her. Leaning over him, she teased him with nibbling kisses, touched, explored, and loved every inch of him. She savored his every ragged breath and soft moan.

When he could stand no more, he reversed their positions with one swift movement. His body flowed over hers. Sliding one hand up the inside of her thigh, he settled into the cradle of her hips.

For a moment, he simply stared down at her face. "God, I love you."

Gazing back at him, she tried to communicate all the love and joy she couldn't seem to express verbally. Capturing his face between her hands, she sealed a silent promise with a deep, demanding kiss.

She was more than he'd ever dreamed, Drew thought hazily. All silken skin and apple blossom scent. His fingers slid into her hair, fanning it out over the pillow as his mouth moved restlessly over hers.

Needing her to become so lost in him that she'd never want to break free, he whispered passionate words against her lips, throat, and breasts. He gave with all the strength and eagerness of a new love, feeling waves of something deeper, more true than he'd ever known before, wash through him.

He lifted his head to gaze down at her. What he saw robbed him of breath and captured his spirit. Need and some jubilant emotion shimmered in her eyes. The brilliance of her smile possessed him.

The miracle of love cascaded through him as he gathered her body into his arms and eased into her warmth. All his senses responded to the exquisite wonder. An aching tenderness twisted his heart. He buried his face in her hair for a moment, then he obeyed the call of each emotion flowing between them.

Caitlin cried out, wrapping herself tightly around him. She felt power rushing over them like a river, carrying them closer and closer to the edge of reason. Vivid shock runners shivered beneath her fevered skin.

Turning her head to one side, she skimmed her lips along his shoulder. The sensuous current of motion and harmony engulfed her. Rapture built and spread like a living flame. It possessed her so completely that for a brief moment in time, as their bodies seemed to explode with ecstasy, she imagined her soul soared free with his.

She held him tightly to her, her legs entwined with his, reluctant to let him go.

Her mind and her heart were so full, she couldn't seem to think clearly. She was certain of only one thing. She was very much in love with an incredibly wonderful man.

Drew watched Caitlin devour the breakfast she'd insisted on serving him in bed. He lifted a disdainfully mocking brow. "How can you stand to eat that stuff?"

"What's wrong with oatmeal cream pies and coffee?" She popped the last bite into her mouth. "Oatmeal is good for you."

"I had something more substantial in mind." He eyed the smear of cream filling on her lower lip, then captured her face between his hands and traced her lips with his tongue.

Lifting his head, he grinned crookedly at her.

"Oatmeal cream pies aren't real food. Read the fine print on the box. They're full of additives and preservatives. But I must say, they taste pretty darn good when you're wearing them."

Pushing him backward, Caitlin draped herself over him, squirming provocatively until she settled into the cradle of his hips. "Haven't you heard of better living through chemistry?" she teased, then turned her attention to exploring his chest with her mouth.

He stroked the satin length of her back. "You must have a thing for cream pies. You're either hitting me with them or feeding them to me."

She stopped kissing his stomach. "Don't mention the pie incident."

"Why not? It's one of my fondest memories." He tangled his fingers in her hair. "Is breakfast over now?"

"You wanted something more substantial." She raised her head and smiled. "So I'm giving it to you."

"Great balls of fire," he sighed as she dipped lower. "I just love breakfast in bed."

The next few weeks passed quickly for Caitlin. Late one afternoon, she drove through the Garden District on her way home from a day of volunteering her services at Riverview's free clinic. Glancing at the scenery, she realized she'd been so caught up in her relationship with Drew, she hadn't noticed the trees were almost bare. Thanksgiving was only a week away.

It wouldn't be long before the damp chill of winter settled in. She smiled, thinking how nice it would be to spend an evening with Drew in front of the fireplace when the weather turned cold enough.

Her smile deepened as she thought of Drew waiting at home for her. She'd never realized how wonderful it was to have someone to go home to. Someone who cared about everything that happened to her while they were apart.

There'd been a lot of time together since Halloween, days and nights of learning to love each other. Their schedules were hectic, but they managed to pack a great deal into their mutual days off.

Being with him was joy for today. They laughed and loved. She didn't think she'd ever been happier.

Except when the nightmare haunted her.

Caitlin stopped at a traffic light. She shivered, remembering the dream that frequently woke her up in a cold sweat in the middle of the night.

In the nightmare, she stood at the bottom of a dark, deep chasm. The only light came from far above its steep walls. Every time she tried to climb up to the light, a soft voice called out to her from the darkness. Indecision paralyzed her as she looked up at the light and listened to the voice.

She knew enough about the psychology of dreams to understand what the nightmare meant. Her subconscious was telling her she would eventually have to make a decision—stay with Drew or follow her own dream.

Behind her, a horn blared impatiently. Startled, Caitlin let out the clutch and eased through the intersection. She abandoned all thoughts of nightmares and indecision as she hurried home to Drew.

When she entered the house, the first thing that caught her attention was a crepe paper streamer dangling from the ceiling in the foyer. She touched the note pinned to it. "Follow the yellow brick road," she read aloud. Puzzled, she glanced down the hallway. A yellow streamer stretched the length of it.

Laughing, she went to the kitchen and dumped the bag of hamburgers on the counter. Then she followed the streamer to the back of the house where it disappeared beneath Drew's closed bedroom door.

What would she find inside the room? she wondered. She pictured the streamer leading to the bed with Drew waiting in the middle, a big yellow bow tied around his waist. She grinned. The man was a romantic, and his imagination was limitless. Visions of a delightful evening danced in her head.

She opened the door and stepped into the room.

He wasn't waiting for her in bed. She sighed in disappointment. He wasn't in there at all as far as she could see.

So what was the point of the yellow streamers? Puzzled, she examined the bedchamber carefully. As she walked farther into the room, she realized something was different.

The difference suddenly clicked in her mind. She froze in place, her eyes wide in shock.

Ten

She saw her mother's colorful pointed-star quilt neatly folded at the foot of Drew's brass bed. It had been on her own bed that morning. Glancing around, she spotted her jewelry box, perfume, and brushes on his dresser. Her vanity table stood in one corner. The silver-framed photograph of her family and the ridiculous *Thing-A-Bob* star head band Drew had bought her in the French Quarter lay on the bedside table.

The shock of discovery hit her full force. A hurricane of emotions swept through her. Drew had moved her belongings into his room—without asking. No discussion. No permission granted. He'd simply arranged her possessions in his bedroom as though he had a right to do so.

Her hands shook on their way up to rest on her hips. Anger billowed in her as disturbing thoughts scampered through her mind.

She should have seen this coming. Every time she gave him an inch, he grabbed it with both hands and tried to stretched it into a mile.

"Hi."

Looking up, she met Drew's eyes in the oval mirror of her vanity table. He was standing behind her, hands tucked deep into the pockets of his jeans. A pleased, boyish grin rested upon his lips.

"Surprised?" he asked in a voice filled with anticipation.

She was quiet for a second, then she turned to face him. "You could say that. Stunned may be closer to what I'm feeling. Even outraged."

His grin faded as Drew looked into her eyes. They were molten gold, a sign he recognized as anger. He hadn't expected that. He stepped toward her.

She backed away. "I wouldn't get too close to me right now if I were you."

He could see her face was taut with anger. "Fine. You want to fight." He walked over to the brass bed and sat down.

"Don't you think you're overreacting?" he went on. "All I've done is save you the trouble of having to do it yourself."

Caitlin took in his calm smile. To her it was an indication he wasn't taking her seriously. Again. "How thoughtful of you to relieve me of that burden." He winced at her sarcastic tone.

She pitched her shoulder bag onto a nearby bentwood rocker, setting it in motion. "Did you even stop to think I might not want to move into your room?"

"Don't you? We're in this bed together every night we're home. I thought we'd reached a silent agreement in the past few weeks."

"I agree that we have a relationship. But, Drew, that doesn't mean you can take charge of my life. I make my own decisions. You can't make them for me and act without regard to my feelings."

She raised her hands in frustration. "By taking it upon yourself to decide it's time for me to move in with you, you've taken away my right to choose. Why didn't you at least discuss it with me?"

He stood and closed the small distance between them. "I didn't realize moving in with me required strategic planning. I thought you'd be happy about it."

"Sometimes you assume too much."

He placed his hands on her shoulders. She allowed the contact, but remained stiff. "Love, I'm thirty years old. Too old to play musical beds. I want you with me. I want to wake up every morning, knowing the first thing I'll see is you lying beside me."

Caitlin saw uncertainty creep into his expression. She also felt herself weakening. Far too often, she found her love for him overruled her common sense.

"We have so little time to be together," he said softly. "I hope you'll make the decision to spend every moment you can with me before . . ." He didn't want to say it aloud. Didn't want to acknowledge the possibility. He still counted on her changing her mind about staying in New Orleans. Although she'd never said she loved him, he knew she did. And if she loved him enough, surely she wouldn't be able to leave him.

He couldn't bring himself to admit she was eventually leaving, Caitlin thought. His past was littered with desertion. Now she understood why he had moved her into his room. It was a subconscious effort to hold her, a way of drawing her deeper into the world he'd created for himself.

She didn't know what to say. In fact, all she really wanted to do was cry. But giving in to tears wasn't her way of dealing with problems. Nor did she simply try to avoid problems in the hope they'd resolve themselves or go away.

"If you want, I'll help you put everything back," he

said. His mask was off, and his expression revealed the very human qualities of vulnerability and hurt.

The last traces of her resistance shattered like fine crystal tossed onto concrete. Caitlin encircled his waist with her arms and rested her cheek against his chest. She felt a desperate need to make things right for him, a need to heal all of his past wounds. A need to make promises for tomorrow. But she couldn't without giving away everything else she wanted in life. No, she couldn't offer false promises, but she could offer him today.

"I suppose you just threw my clothes in your closet," she murmured, rising up on her toes. She pressed her lips to the warm hollow of his throat. His quick intake of breath told her he was surprised by her surrender.

Drawing her closer, he dropped a kiss on her forehead. "No, I hung them up nice and neat."

Slipping his hands under her arms, he lifted her off her feet. His mouth sought hers in a hard, possessive kiss as he walked backward. When he reached the bed, he fell onto it, taking her with him. His fingers parted the curtain of her hair which flowed over them both. The nature of the kiss changed to a taunting, teasing intensity that flooded him with a miracle of sweetness and pleasure.

With an easy rolling movement, he reversed their positions, covering her with the blanket of his body and its feverish heat. He raised his head to look into her eyes. They were overbright, shining up at him. The sensitive tips of her fingers brushed strokes of color and life into his cheeks. Her breath was warm and intoxicating upon his skin.

He kissed her gently, then said, "I love you, Catie."

The day before Thanksgiving, Caitlin stood on the sidewalk on St. Charles Avenue, staring up at a three-story, eighty-year-old house. After inspecting it for over an hour, she couldn't believe Drew was actually considering the property for his multidisciplinary practice.

"I told you it was perfect, shrimp bait. Don't you just love it?" He wrapped his arm around her neck and gave her a playful hug.

She looked at him skeptically. "Sure it's perfect. A perfect money pit. Drew, that building is in bad shape. It's going to cost you a fortune."

"It has character. Didn't you notice its bracketed entablatures? The roof is French second empire mansard."

"Trust me," she said dryly, "bracketed entablatures aren't worth that kind of money. Find a building with no character. Your banker will have heart failure if you buy that run-down mausoleum."

"Use your imagination, Catie. Think of the possibilities. There's enough space in the back for a parking lot and a play area for kids. The structure of the house is sound. We'll have to do a little updating. Make some changes like rewiring, put in an elevator, make it handicap accessible, divide some of the larger rooms into smaller ones. But I think we can do it without destroying the integrity of the architecture."

Frowning, Caitlin pulled away. "*We?* As in you and your so far nonexistent partners?"

"We as in you and me." He reached for her hand and kissed her knuckles.

"No." She shook her head. "I've said no countless times in a loud, clear voice. I do not want to go into private practice. Why do you persist in deluding yourself about it?"

He tightened his hold on her hand. "None of your applications for research work have panned out. Catie love, I'm simply trying to make you see you have another option. Do what you've been trained to do, for Pete's sake."

She fought to keep her temper under control. Had he brought her there hoping she'd adore the place and instantly change her mind about her life's work?

Tugging to free her hand, she said, "I haven't heard from Houston yet. And I'm not desperate enough to change my mind or sink good money into a questionable piece of property."

He ignored her last statement. "What if you get a negative response from Houston?"

Her chin went up. "I'll reapply next year. By then I'll be board certified, and that may make all the difference."

"And what will you do in the meantime? Are you going to waste an entire year, waiting for something that might not happen?"

"I can work in Riverview's free clinic."

Drew's face felt tight with strain. He forced a smile to mask his inner turmoil. "Well, you have to decide what's best for you."

"That's right, I do."

In silence, they walked to his car and got in. Before starting the engine, he turned to her. "If you don't mind, I want to stop by the hospital to check on Joey Anderson. He's had a few rough nights lately. He caught a cold last week, and with his poor immune system, I'm worried about it developing into pneumonia."

Caitlin studied his defensive expression. In the past two months, he'd spent a great deal of time with the little boy, even sitting with him several nights when volunteers failed to show up. Every time she tried to talk to him about the potential dangers of the situation, he impatiently dismissed her concerns.

"All right," she said, not wanting to start another argument. "Let's go visit Joey."

• • •

Christmas mistletoe hung in every room. Brushing her hair to glowing perfection, Caitlin looked up and grinned. She couldn't even visit the bathroom without finding a sprig dangling over her head. Sweeping one side of her hair upward, she anchored it just above her ear with two rhinestone hairpins.

She stepped back and gave herself a critical once-over. The red silk dress, an early Christmas present from Drew, was held up by three thin diagonal straps on one shoulder and fit tightly to her waist. Her only jewelry was the rhinestone hairpins and a pair of fake diamond earrings.

Feeling exotically feminine and ready to seduce Drew beyond all rational thought, she left the bathroom to finish preparing her special pre-Christmas Eve dinner.

In the kitchen, she covered her dress with an apron, then assembled the ingredients for a spinach salad. As she worked, she occasionally glanced out the window above the sink.

It would be dark soon, and Drew still wasn't home. Several hours ago, he'd made quite a production of going on some mysterious errand. His aim, she thought with a smile, had been to pique her curiosity. He'd achieved his objective. She was dying to know what he was up to.

After she finished the salad, she checked on the progress of the rest of the meal. She wanted everything to be perfect for their first Christmas celebration.

She thought of the gift she planned to give him that night. It was something money couldn't buy. And she could hardly wait to see his face when she gave it to him.

Two hours later, Caitlin sat across the candlelit

dining room table from Drew. She tried not to appear too nervous as he picked up his fork for a first taste of the meal she'd carefully planned.

Drew eyed the crepe-wrapped Veal Lafayette on his plate. It looked good and smelled delicious. However, being well acquainted with Caitlin's limited culinary skills, he knew looks and smells could be deceiving.

Well aware that she was anxiously anticipating his opinion, he put on a pleasant expression. He was determined to like her dinner even if it killed him. This was their first Christmas celebration, and in honor of it, he'd donned the charcoal-blue dinner jacket and trousers with the tartan silk cummerbund he wore only to fancy Mardi Gras balls.

He cut into the crepe and took a bite. Utter surprise reflected on his face. "This is good. Really outstanding. Catie, I'm impressed."

Laughing, she picked up her own fork. "You don't have to make it sound like I can't boil water."

"I know you can. I've seen you drop bags of frozen entrées into it. I'm just saying that for a woman whose idea of culinary delight is Lean Cuisine, this is an incredible meal."

"I'll ignore the slings and arrows and accept the compliment. However, I'm trying to do a great deal more than impress you with food." She swept a lingering gaze over him, thinking how beautifully masculine he looked in his evening attire. "I'm trying to seduce you."

He grinned. "You're in luck. I love being seduced. Especially by women in hot red dresses. Did I buy that dress for you?" he teased.

"You know you did."

An odd, disquieting expression lingered in his eyes. "I like buying you things. Remember that. I'd give you anything you wanted if you'd let me."

He watched her look away at his serious tone.

Uncertainty struck him. She found it difficult to accept gifts from him, and rarely did, except for simple, inexpensive things. He considered what he'd done that day and doubt formed a lump in his throat.

Her voice, light and teasing, broke the silence. "In that case, I've always wanted my own island."

"What would you do with an island?"

"Oh, I don't know. Collect seashells and make tacky souvenirs out of them. I'd sell them to the shops in the French Market."

He laughed and helped himself to another serving of veal. "You'd be bored within a week's time. What else would you do if you could do anything or have anything you wanted?"

She smiled dreamily. "Rent Disney World for a day and make myself sick on rides and junk food."

"Personally, I prefer your island idea. I can see two people, me and you, alone on a deserted tropical paradise. Brings to mind a few great fantasies."

"Like what?"

His gaze held hers for a moment in the flickering candlelight. "Like chasing each other around naked all day."

"And moaning all night with third-degree sun-burns?"

"Not in my fantasy. We'd turn golden brown and make love by the lagoon."

A soft, loving smile curved her lips. "I'm not certain who's seducing whom tonight."

She pushed back her chair. "Shall we have dessert in the living room by the fireplace?"

"Perfect. What's for dessert?"

"Oatmeal cream pies," she said with a straight face, then laughed at his pained expression. "Actually, I'm going to attempt Bananas Foster."

"Is the fire extinguisher working?" He grinned in

response to her mock-offended look. "Just kidding," he said, following her to the kitchen.

Caitlin managed to ignite the banana and rum liqueurs without incident. They loaded a tray and headed for the living room. Before reaching their destination, Drew stopped her twice to take advantage of the mistletoe dangling from open doorways.

Sitting on the floor by the blazing fireplace, they consumed the dessert while listening to Renaissance Christmas music. The fire popped and crackled, giving off color illusions of cold blue, soft amber, orange and gold.

Comfortably satiated, Caitlin stretched out on the Oriental carpet, placing her head in Drew's lap. Her gaze wandered to the Christmas tree in the corner.

They had decorated the tree with colorful lights, painted gingerbread people, and her mother's delicately crocheted snowflakes. A golden-haired porcelain angel with silk wings benevolently graced the top.

Under the tree were several presents from her to Drew. But the one she wanted to give him that night wasn't boxed and wrapped in pretty paper. *I love you.* She silently savored the words bonded to her mind, heart, and spirit.

Many times over the past two months, she'd wanted to say those words, but somehow they'd always lodged in her throat, never making it past the barrier of her lips. For her, the words themselves were a promise and a commitment.

Drew traced the curve of her cheek, delighting in the way her smooth skin felt against his fingers. The firelight reflected in her eyes, making them appear more amber than usual. She seemed quiet, not withdrawn but thoughtful, as though carefully weighing some decision.

"What are you thinking about?" he asked softly. "You have a very mysterious look in your eyes."

She brushed a lock of hair back from his forehead. Now was the time, she decided, for her gift. "I was just thinking about how much I love you."

Drew froze. Had she just said what he could swear he heard? "Do you mind repeating that?" His voice was a hoarse whisper.

Taking his hand, she brought it to her mouth and pressed a kiss into his palm. "I love you. Merry Christmas."

He shook his head, feeling dazed. "I was beginning to think I'd never hear you say you loved me." He pulled her upright to sit on his lap and held her tight. "Say it again."

"I love you." Touching her lips to his, she sealed her gift with everything in her heart and soul.

Drew drank in the love she poured into that kiss. Everything was going to be fine, he thought. They had a future together. *Forever.*

Now he knew she would accept his own gift. Eager to give it to her, he lifted his mouth from hers. "I have a present for you," he blurted out. "I didn't know if it was the right thing or not, but now—"

He lifted her onto the floor and got to his feet. "Stay right there. Don't move."

She laughed. "This wouldn't have anything to do with that secret errand you made such a big production of this afternoon, would it?"

"You'll see." He was smiling as he left the room.

Caitlin shook her head. Drew and his surprises. He delighted over giving and receiving them. Sometimes she wondered if he'd never gotten surprises when he was a child. Perhaps that was why he enjoyed them so much.

He came back in with his hands behind his back. "Close your eyes."

"All right. But if I feel a rubber snake down my back, the seduction is off."

"No fear, love." He placed something on her lap. "You can look now."

She slowly opened her eyes. Glancing down, she saw some sort of document rolled up and tied with a red ribbon.

Puzzled, she looked at Drew. He sat on his heels in front of her, very still. The expression on his face was two parts excitement, one part anxiety.

She untied the ribbon, then she carefully unrolled the papers and spread them out. Quickly she scanned the legal document. Shock slapped at her like powerful ocean waves.

Her mind reeled. The contract in her hand listed her as co-purchaser of the St. Charles Avenue property. Trying to remain calm, she met his eager gaze. "I can't accept this."

"Of course you can," he said, settling onto his knees. "I know you're surprised. But I just knew you'd change your mind." Smiling, he continued, "If we start now, we'll have the property in shape for business this fall."

He cupped her chin tenderly in his warm hand. "I love you, Catie mine." He covered her mouth with his.

It took a few seconds for him to realize she wasn't kissing him back. He lifted his head and saw that her eyes were filled with pain, not the pleasure of surprise.

He watched her drop the contract on the floor as if it burned her fingers. Icy fear twisted in his gut. He could almost feel the tension in her body. It seemed to invade the room, crackling and shimmering like fire.

His eyes narrowed with concern. "What's wrong? Why are you acting like this?"

Caitlin felt herself trembling. She crossed her arms

over her waist as if she could hold back the tide of emotions threatening to drown her. "I love you with all my heart," she said. "But that doesn't mean I want my name on that contract. My God, Drew, I don't have that kind of money."

Relief washed over him, and he smiled. "The money isn't a problem," he said, placing his hands on her shoulders. "You worry over the craziest things. You don't have to spend a penny to finance our project. After all, when we're married, everything I have will be yours too."

He saw the blood drain from her face. Her body went rigid beneath his hands.

"You're doing it again." Her voice came out a hallow whisper. "You've worked it all out in your mind, planned to the last detail. We'll buy the property. Fix it up. Get married. Go into practice together. But you didn't ask me. You just expect me to blindly accept the way you envision our lives."

He blew out an impatient breath, letting go of her so he could run his fingers through his hair. "All right. Catie, marry me. Share the property with me and become my partner."

"That sounds more like a demand than a proposal. We have to talk this over. I can't make major decisions like that on the spur of the moment. I can't impulsively say yes without weighing the consequences."

"Can't or won't?"

Several seconds of raw silence passed. Looking at him became painful. She glanced away.

"You said you loved me. That changes everything."

She met his gaze. "It doesn't change what I want to do with my life. It doesn't mean I'll automatically fall in with everything you want. The multidisciplinary practice is your dream, not mine. You are fortunate.

You have the financial ability to establish your career anywhere you please."

His eyes narrowed. "New Orleans is my home. I belong here. I can't set up my practice anywhere else."

"Can't or won't?" she asked, throwing his own question back at him. She held up her hand to stop him from speaking. "Don't worry. I'm not asking you to leave your precious city. I'm just trying to make you understand that I have to go where the opportunity lies."

Drew stood up. He walked over to the fireplace and gazed down into the flames. How could she say she loved him one minute, then the next minute reject the perfect solution that would allow them to stay together?

"It's been years since I've let anyone get close enough to hurt me," he said. He turned to face her. "I don't know what else to say to you except I love you."

He started walking out of the room.

"Where are you going?" she cried, rising to her knees.

"Out. I need to think."

Stunned, she got to her feet and followed him into the foyer. "Drew, we need to talk."

"Not now, Catie," he said, wrenching the front door open. "I've have enough *discussing* things with you tonight."

"We haven't discussed anything. Please—"

He stalked out and slammed the door behind him.

Caitlin drew in an unsteady breath, willing herself not to cry. Crying wouldn't help. Her eyes burning with unshed tears, she walked back down the hallway.

She entered the bedroom she shared with Drew and went through the motions of undressing. Unable to remember ever feeling so weary or defeated, she sank down on the bed.

It was dark as a tomb when Caitlin awoke with a start. She identified the sound that had wakened her and softly called out, "Drew?"

"Sorry, love. I didn't mean to wake you." The mattress gave slightly as he got into bed.

She instinctively reached for him. "Are you all right? I was so worried about you." His arms went around her. She felt no restraint or uncertainty in his touch, only a desperate need, a mutual acceptance of something necessary to them both.

He kissed her temple. "I'm okay. I'm sorry, Catie mine. No, don't say anything," he said, drawing away from the fingers she placed upon his lips to stop his apology. "I know I assumed a great deal tonight, and I shouldn't have. I just want it all, Catie. I want what you've had all your life. A real home with a warm, openly affectionate family. I want that with you."

"Oh, Drew." She closed her eyes against the threat of tears. Her hand trembled as she stroked his hair. "I understand how you feel. I don't want to hurt you. But there are things I have to do on my own. Things you can't do for me or buy for me."

"I know that. But I can't help wishing this situation wasn't so damn complicated. It's like constantly waiting for the other shoe to drop."

"I wish it wasn't either. But it is. We have to deal with that. Until I hear from Houston, I can't make any concrete plans. I love you, but I cannot compromise what I want to do with my life without losing my self-respect."

"Okay," he said after a long pause. "I don't like it, but I can understand what you're saying."

"Falling in love wasn't something I envisioned for

myself at this point in my career. I honestly don't know what to do about it."

"Love doesn't accommodate personal agendas," he agreed. "It just sneaks up and kicks you in the butt." He smiled faintly. "Or hits you in the face with a pie."

"I can see I'm never going to live that down." She lovingly ran her hand along his arm to entwine her fingers with his.

"Nope." Humor fled from his voice. "What are we going to do?"

"I don't know." Her own voice was unsteady. "Just love each other, I guess. Take it one day at—" She couldn't continue without succumbing to the sobs building in her throat. She buried her face in the curve of his neck.

She was crying, he thought bleakly. Hell, he felt like shedding a few tears himself. He kissed the top of her head. "It's all right," he lied. "Things have a way of working out."

She shifted, half covering his body with hers.

He inhaled sharply and held her closer. Pain filled him, and he was glad the darkness hid his expression from her.

She raised her head. "Drew, I have to know. Where does a man go to think when he's formally dressed in black tie and tartan cummerbund?"

Her unexpected question made him laugh. "I drove around town for a while. Then I went to the hospital."

"Bet that caused a stir." She kissed his neck.

"One of the residents laughed himself silly. Got a few whistles, though, when I passed by the nurses' station."

"The hussies," she teased. "Why did you end up there?"

He shrugged. "Didn't know where else to go. Thought I might as well check on Joey."

An alarm sounded in her mind. "Drew, I hate to say

it, but I'm concerned about you getting too involved with one patient. I'm afraid you're losing your objectivity."

"You worry too much. If I thought there was any danger of that, I'd assign his case to someone else."

Not wanting to start another argument, she let it drop. "How is Joey?"

Drew's arms tightened around her. "Not good. I don't want to talk about it right now." He gently eased her onto her back. "I'd rather make love to you."

"I do believe I owe you a seduction," she murmured.

Eleven

Caitlin sat alone in the kitchen, lingering over a late breakfast as she stared out the window at the dreary weather the new year had brought in. Wishing Drew would hurry home, she sighed and picked up her coffee cup.

He was at the hospital. On his day off. He'd been doing that a lot lately. She didn't know whether he was using work as an escape from their problems, or if he was simply too involved with Joey Anderson. Either way, she was very concerned.

Since the night of their pre-Christmas celebration and confrontation, an element of quiet desperation had infiltrated their relationship. It was with them when they made love. It crept into their careful conversations. They treated each other like fragile glass. On the surface they were so genial and kind, it sometimes made her feel a little heartsick.

It was as if the complications they faced didn't exist, but those complications were never far from her mind. She suspected it was the same for him.

Her nightmare of standing in the dark chasm came

with alarming frequency. She didn't know how much longer she could go on with the pretense that their problems would resolve themselves.

Eventually, she would have to make a choice. The man she loved was firmly rooted, present and future, in a place she would have to leave if she chose to pursue her own goals. It was tearing her apart emotionally.

Feeling sadder than the gray January sky, she got up to refill her cup. The phone rang before she reached the coffeepot. She set the cup down and answered the call.

"Hello? Yes, I'm Dr. MacKenzie."

A man introduced himself as Dr. Leon Henderson, Director of the Human Development and Research Institute in Houston, Texas.

Her heart hammered in her chest. Excitement and hope shot up like fireworks in her head. She almost stopped breathing when he praised her credentials and asked if she would come to Houston for an interview.

"Yes, Dr. Henderson, Monday would be fine." She was amazed she could sound so calm when inside she was jumping up and down like an excited kid.

"Great," he said. "Just give my secretary, Mrs. Bateman, a call to confirm the date. She'll make your travel arrangements. The Institute will pay your expenses of course."

She grabbed a pen and notepad from the counter and quickly jotted down the phone number he recited.

A few minutes later, she slowly replaced the receiver. She tore off the top sheet and tossed the pad and pencil onto the counter. Then she leaned against the refrigerator and stared at the number written on the paper.

A chance. She had a chance. After all her planning, hoping, and disappointments, she had a chance. Hallelujah! A thrilled squeak erupted from her throat.

Her legs began to shake. She slid down the refrigerator's smooth surface and sat on the floor.

"What are you doing, shrimp bait?" Drew asked in an amused tone.

Color drained from her face. In her excitement, she hadn't heard him come into the house. She lifted her head and gazed up at him.

When he saw how pale she was, his amusement turned to concern. "Are you all right?" He knelt down on one knee beside her.

"I . . . I think I need a hug," she stammered.

He sat down and pulled her into his lap. Her head dropped onto his shoulder, and she placed one hand over his heart.

He could feel her trembling. "It's all right, love." Seriously alarmed, he gently rocked her back and forth. "Talk to me."

Caitlin's mind was spinning. The opportunity she'd dreamed about, waited for, prayed for, was being offered to her. Her chance of a lifetime was out there. She couldn't see, feel, or touch it. Yet it was almost as dear to her as the heart beating beneath her hand. Her fingers slid upward. His face felt warm and slightly rough against her palm.

"Catie, you're scaring me. Are you sick? Are you pregnant?" A small seed of hope flourished in his mind. Although they'd been careful about using precautions, nothing was completely foolproof.

"No. I'm not sick or pregnant," she finally said in a shaky voice. She tightly clutched the notepaper she still held in her hand as tension knotted in her stomach. There was no easy way of telling him. She raised her head to look at his face and willed herself to remain calm.

"I just got a call from the Director of the Human Development and Research Institute in Houston. They want to interview me. On Monday."

Drew stared at her. A dull ache throbbed at his temple. Not trusting himself to speak, he inclined his head in a stiff nod.

"I told Dr. Henderson—he's the director—that I'm interested in the position. I'm going for the interview."

She saw dismay creep into the brilliant green eyes she loved. Nervously, she thrust her fingers through her hair, sweeping it back from her face.

A brittle silence stretched between them.

Although the room's temperature was pleasant, and she wore a thick pullover sweater and jeans, Caitlin suddenly felt cold. Panicked thoughts filled her head. Though he still held her in a loose embrace, she could feel Drew slipping away from her. Forcing herself to meet his eyes, she saw them cloud over with a hard iciness.

Something inside her shattered. Coldness was an emotion she'd never seen in his gaze before. At least, not when he was looking at her. She laid one hand over his and flinched when he shied away from her touch.

She got up and walked over to the sink, staring out the window above it. After stuffing the sheet of paper into her pocket, she crossed her arms protectively over her chest.

"What about us?" Drew's quiet voice was edged with steel.

Gaze locked on a barren oak tree outside, she said, "It's an interview, not an offer."

"I'll ask you again, Caitlin. *What about us?*"

"I don't have an answer." She whirled to face him. "We both knew this could happen."

A look of discomfort passed over his handsome face. Anger glazed inside her as she slowly realized the truth. "You were hoping Houston would turn me down. Weren't you?"

He stood. His expression changed to a mask of stone.

"Weren't you?" she said louder.

"Yes, dammit." He strode over to her and caught hold of her shoulders.

Her vision blurred. "That's not fair." She blinked back tears.

"Is it fair for you to run out on the commitment we've made to each other?" he asked grimly. "We *are* committed. It may not be legally binding. We may not have a piece of paper to prove it. But we are *committed*. You can't skip off to Texas and ignore it."

"Skip off to Texas?" She reached up to shove his hands away. "Don't you know this is tearing me apart? I don't want to have to choose between you and my career."

"But you're going to," he said bitterly.

"Why should I be the one to give up everything I want? Not once have you considered changing your plans, but you expect me to change mine."

She slammed her palm against the wall. "This is just a house, Drew, not a holy shrine. You've planted your feet on a piece of real estate. A damn piece of real estate. That's all it is. *You* are choosing it over me."

The words hung in the air between them.

Drew stood absolutely rigid until an odd stricken look passed like a shadow over his face.

In a flash of intuition, Caitlin knew she was seeing into the private hell of a man coming face-to-face with a dilemma he could not control.

Her anger faded enough for her to feel the pain of her heart breaking. "I do love you," she said softly.

"Sure." His voice was flat, expressionless. "For now."

Early Tuesday evening, Caitlin followed the stream of passengers off the airplane and along the ramp to the gate area. Her legs were shaky. A knot of emotion clogged her throat. She identified the sensation as fear. A fighting-for-your-life kind of feeling accompanied each step she took.

Would Drew be waiting for her? Would he be the cool, distant stranger she'd left Monday morning?

She shifted her wool coat from one arm to the other, then nervously tugged the cuffs of her pin-striped suit jacket into place.

Her eyes flickered over the crowd. She saw him before he noticed her. Even in a crowd, she noted with a hint of pride, he had an innately captivating presence.

He must have come straight from the hospital, she thought. He wore a white lab jacket over gray flannel slacks, a pink shirt, and a slim preppy tie. She smiled. She liked the fact he was bold enough to wear pink. He looked completely comfortable and masculine in that color.

Drew glanced around the gate area, searching the crowd for Caitlin. When he saw her, she was smiling in his direction. He felt the warmth of that smile reach across the sea of people and touch him.

He was starved for the sight of her. She'd been away for thirty-five hours and some odd minutes. It seemed like a lifetime to him.

Suddenly her bright smile faded. She became solemn.

A sense of dread filled him, and he pushed his way through the throng to get to her.

Seeing him move with swift grace toward her, Caitlin straightened her shoulders and propelled herself forward to meet him.

They stopped within inches of each other and stared.

She became painfully aware of the reserved expression in his eyes. An eternity seemed to pass before she found herself enveloped in his arms.

Drew lifted his head and looked down at her face, his gaze fixing on her eyes. Alert to any inflection in their autumn-colored depths, he read love and tenderness there, touched with pain.

"They offered you the position." It wasn't a question. It was a statement he could read in her eyes.

"Yes." Her voice was barely audible but steady.

"You accepted."

Her heart constricted in her chest. "Not formally."

"But you will."

"Yes."

"Well, I guess that's it. We've both made our decisions. Now we just have to live with them."

"Drew, please . . ." Caitlin closed her eyes for a second. What could she say? He was right. Decisions had been made. They'd have to live with the consequences.

She opened her eyes, knowing they revealed her profound regret. "I missed you so much."

He leaned down to place a gentle kiss upon her lips. "I missed you too. Come on, I'll take you out to dinner. We'll . . . celebrate."

He took her to a restaurant in the Garden District. Soon they were up to their knuckles in big bowls of barbecued shrimp. The sauce was spicy hot and delicious, but neither of them ate very much. The waited finally took away their half-eaten meals and poured coffee into their cups.

"The food is excellent here," Caitlin said, though she could barely remember how anything tasted.

Drew murmured agreement and handed her a hot towel scented with lemon water.

She wiped the thick sauce from her fingers, her gaze never wavering from him. He looked tired. She noted the dark circles beneath his eyes.

Drawing in a deep breath, she garnered all of her strength and courage. "I love you more than I ever thought possible, Drew." She leaned forward. "I don't know what to do about us."

He picked up his cup and took a sip of the chicory-flavored coffee. She couldn't decipher what he was thinking behind his hooded eyes and unreadable expression.

"I cannot refuse the opportunity the Institute is offering me," she went on. "And yet, I don't want to throw away everything we have together."

Drew searched her face. She held his gaze so beseechingly. It was as if she thought he had a solution to their problem hidden amid the plastic rings, sugarless gum, and magic tricks in his pockets.

His brows knit together. He held out one hand, palm up, in a helpless gesture. He couldn't magically produce an answer for her. He didn't have one.

"What do you want from me, Catie? Absolution for leaving? Fine. You've got it. Go with my blessing." His voice was caustic, and he hated it. But he felt as though he were bleeding from every pore.

"My back is against the wall," he continued. "If you want me to beg you to stay, forget it. I don't beg anymore. You have your research program waiting for you in Houston. I have a building on St. Charles Avenue waiting to be remodeled. Give me a break. I don't have a magic solution to make either of those things or the miles between them disappear."

He signaled the waiter and pulled his wallet out of his pocket. Choosing a credit card, he flipped it onto the table.

Caitlin sat back. Lowering her head, she stared at her folded hands. Guilt and anger stung her.

She waited until the waiter had collected the credit card and moved away before looking up again.

Drew sat sideways, one arm draped over the back of his chair. His gaze was trained on the photographs of celebrities on the wall. He stared at them as if fascinated by the sight of such notables having dined in the same restaurant. But she knew he couldn't have cared less.

"Would it be easier for you if I moved out?" she asked. "I guess I could stay with Debbie Wilson for a while." It killed her soul to say that. Every nerve in her body stood at attention, waiting for his answer.

He nailed her to her chair with a sharp glare. "Hell no. Don't be stupid, Caitlin. I'll take whatever time we have left."

Frustrated and hurt, he ran his fingers through his hair. "Look, I admit you've been offered a wonderful opportunity," he said in a gentler tone. "I am proud of you. But at the moment, I don't feel noble or unselfish enough to be happy about it. Give me some time to adjust. Between now and July, maybe we can find some way to resolve this problem. I don't relish the idea of a long-distance relationship. God know's I've had enough of them to last me a lifetime. But it may be our only choice."

Before she could say anything, his beeper demanded his attention. She watched him shut it off, then without a word, he pushed back his chair and left the table in search of a phone.

The waiter returned and placed the bill and credit card on the table. She shook her head when he asked if they needed anything else.

When Drew came back, he signed the receipt and pocketed the card. "Let's go."

She rose, removed her coat from the chair next to her, and slipped it on.

Neither of them spoke as they left the restaurant.

Outside frigid night air touched her face. She shivered. Stumbling over an uneven section of sidewalk, she would have fallen if not for his steadying hand on her arm.

Once they were settled in the car, she peered at his shadowed profile. "Is it Joey?"

He started the engine. "Yes." His tone was brusque.

"Is something wrong? I thought you said his condition had stabilized."

"He's recovering from his bout with pneumonia. With a little luck, he'll be going home in a week or two. We'll continue his treatments on an out-patient basis."

"Oh, then you don't have to go in tonight," she said with relief.

"Yes, I do. Joey's upset about something. He's been crying so hard, he's having trouble breathing. The resident on call gave him oxygen to regulate his breathing and calm him down. I'm going in to sit with him for a while."

"Do you really think that's necessary?"

Drew's hands tightened on the steering wheel. He met her concerned gaze with a cool stare that told her he knew best how to handle his own patient.

He pulled away from the curb and lurched into the traffic.

Huddling inside her coat to combat both the external and internal cold, Caitlin bit her lower lip to keep from starting another argument.

When he turned onto their street, she could no longer remain silent. "Drew," she began nervously.

He glanced at her, then looked back to the dimly lit street.

"I need to say something you aren't going to like, but you have to stop and think. Evaluate—"

"Dammit, Caitlin, you're not moving out! I will not fight with you about it now. I do not have the time or the energy."

"I wasn't going to say anything about moving out, so don't yell at me."

"I'm sorry, shrimp bait." He let out a tired sigh. "I

didn't mean to snap your head off. But every time I turn around lately, I'm running into a brick wall. I have all the pressure I can handle at the moment. Whatever is going through your head, save it for later."

"It's not about us. I want to talk to you about Joey. You're too close to that child. You've lost your objectivity. You can't tell me that if you'd received the same call about one of your other patients, you'd be rushing off to the hospital. The situation with Joey has been taken care of. He's okay for the night. It isn't necessary for you to sit with him. Have you given any thought to what you're doing in allowing him to become emotionally dependent on you?"

Drew's jaw ached from his clenching his teeth together. "Dr. MacKenzie, I wouldn't presume to tell you how to treat your patients. Do not interfere with mine."

He stopped the car in front of the house. "Do you have your keys?" he asked tersely.

"Drew." She laid her hand on his shoulder and felt him tense. He wouldn't look at her.

"Don't wait up for me. I don't know when I'll be home."

She tried to get through to him one more time. "You're chief resident of pediatrics. If you discovered one of your residents or interns was personally involved with a patient, you'd set him straight. You know you would reassign the patient to someone else. You have to let go."

Her harping on his supposed loss of objectivity made him stiff with rage. He simply reacted. Reaching over her, he wrenched the door open. "Get out." Cold finality edged his voice.

Stunned, Caitlin stared at him for a second. Then she flung herself out of the car and slammed the door.

She stood on the sidewalk, feeling numb as he drove off.

Twelve

Through a narrow slit in the curtains, faint streaks of dawn slipped into the hospital room.

Drew sat slumped in a hard vinyl chair. He ran a hand over his face. His eyes were gritty from lack of sleep. He hadn't felt so exhausted mentally and physically since his internship eons ago.

He glanced at the bed.

Joey slept peacefully, his frail body curled up next to the guardrail. His slumber had been undisturbed by respiratory problems or dreams.

In contrast, Drew had spent the night locked in a nightmare of reflection and self-recrimination. He'd reached into the dark corners of his mind and evaluated his actions with stark honesty.

Now he was left with one thought. He loved Caitlin MacKenzie. Loved her more than anything or anyone. Without her, his future was bleak and lonely.

Drew eased himself out of the chair and walked over to the sink. He splashed cold water on his face, then blindly grabbed a paper towel and dried off.

He gave the sleeping child one last glance before he left the room.

In the corridor, he stood for a moment letting his eyes adjust to the bright light. Exhaustion hit him. Closing his eyes, he leaned against the wall. Perhaps, he thought, he ought to beg a cup of coffee from the nursing staff before he went home.

He felt a tug on the hem of his lab jacket. Looking down, he found a pair of solemn brown eyes staring up at him. Those eyes belonged to the little sprite named Mary, whom everyone called Zoo.

"Hi, Dr. Drew," she said shyly.

"Well, good morning, Miss Zoo." He managed a smile. "You're up awfully early. Do the nurses know you've escaped from the ward?"

Her satiny brown face dimpled in a conspirator's grin. "Not yet. You won't tell, will you?"

He shook his head and crossed his heart.

The child studied him for a moment, then frowned. She hung her head and stared at the bunny slippers on her feet. "Why don't you like me anymore?"

Drew started, becoming blind and deaf to the chatter of two orderlies pushing mops across the floor only a few yards away. He knelt down to Zoo's eye level. "I like you. We're buddies."

Zoo squirmed, scuffing the toe of one slipper against the tile. "Well . . . you don't say funny stuff no more. And you hardly ever come play with us in the Sun Room."

Drew paled at the unconscious reprimand in the child's simple statement. He swallowed a large lump of recrimination.

"I'm sorry, Zoo. I guess I haven't been in a very funny mood lately. Have I been terribly grumpy?"

"Yeah. I got a new game. My grandpa gave it to me. It's real fun."

He couldn't resist the hope shining in her beautiful brown eyes. "I'm off today. But I'll play it with you tomorrow."

"For true?"

He smiled. She always wanted to know if a promise was for true. The other kind, she'd once said to him, was too easy to break.

"For true, little Zoo. I'll play with you and all your friends too," he solemnly stated in Dr. Seuss fashion.

"Oh, boy!" She spun on her heels. " 'Bye, Dr. Drew."

He shoved his hands in his pockets and watched the little girl until she disappeared around corner.

From the mouths of a child and a woman who loved him, he thought wearily. Each had stated her concern in a different way, but both obviously had come to the same conclusion. He was too involved with one patient.

Why had he gone above and beyond the normal call of duty with Joey Anderson? Empathy maybe. He felt a strange kinship with the boy. Joey reminded him of himself at the same age. They both knew what it felt like to be so frightened, yet so determined to show the world a smiling nothing-bothers-me facade.

It was time, Drew told himself, to say good-bye to many things. To Joey, to past insecurities, to pieces of real estate.

He let his internal automatic pilot take over and lead him toward the elevator. He wanted to go home, curl up beside Catie, and let her heal his bruised spirit.

When he got home, he found her in the living room. She was wrapped in a blanket, asleep on the sofa. From the smudges of mascara on her cheeks, he knew she'd been crying.

He sat down in the nearby Queen Anne chair, propped his elbow on the armrest, and cupped his chin in his hand. For a long time, he simply gazed at her, loving with his eyes every soft curve, every plane and angle of her sweet face.

Then he looked around at the place he'd come to

call home. Without her in it, it was just walls, windows, and material possessions. The only home he really needed was in her heart.

Hearing her stir and moan softly, he glanced back to the sofa. Her eyes blinked open, and she frowned in confusion.

"Good morning, love."

Her gaze found his. Her eyes seemed to bore into him as if she were trying to see his soul. She was his soul. He'd have to tell her that sometime."

Time. He wanted a lifetime with her. All he had to do was reach out and accept it.

He opened his arms wide. "Come here, Catie."

Without speaking, she threw off the blanket, got up, and walked toward him. When she reached him, he drew her down onto his lap wrapped his arms around her.

"Home isn't a place," she murmured. She pressed a delicate kiss to his lips, then buried her face in the curve of his neck.

He was startled to hear her speak aloud a thought so similar to his own of a few minutes ago. All he could say was, "I beg your pardon?"

"Home is a feeling that comes from here," she said, placing her hand over his heart. "It's being with people who love you. Drew, I know how much you love New Orleans, but you and I love each other more. We can make a home anywhere."

She raised her head, letting him see the love and vulnerability in her eyes. "Please think about it. I want to marry you and make a home for the two of us in Houston."

Emotion clogged his throat. After all the times they'd fought about that very subject, he knew it had taken great deal of courage for her to ask him that. But she loved him and she was willing to risk rejection. He felt humbled.

Taking her face between his hands, he pressed a tender kiss upon her mouth. "I accept. If you hadn't asked, I was planning to follow you to Houston and camp out on your doorstep until you took pity on me."

Her heart swelled with love. "Oh, Drew, I was so afraid you'd say no."

His eyes filled with tender passion. "I spent most of the night coming to terms with myself. I just couldn't envision being happy without you. You were right when you said I was choosing a piece of real estate over you. Just as you were right about Joey. I'm turning his case over to another resident."

He kissed away a tear that slid down her cheek. "With you, home could be in the middle of an iceberg for all I care. Home is a feeling. I want to dwell in it with you always."

"Hold me," she whispered. "Love me."

"I do love you."

He maneuvered them both onto the floor, and they slowly undressed each other. Joy sparkled in her eyes and was echoed in his. Soft endearments and promises accompanied their caressing hands. They merged as one and allowed the flame of passion to drive them onward.

Afterward, Caitlin lay atop him, savoring the tranquility flowing between them.

"I'm sorry about the St. Charles property," she said. "I know how much it meant to you."

He shrugged. "It's a wonderful old relic. But I'd rather lose it than you. Let's make a weekend trip to Houston soon and scout out some possible building sites."

He smiled and feathered a kiss across her forehead. His sense of humor suddenly came out of hiding. "When you gave me my just desserts, did you ever think it would lead to this?"

She groaned. "You're never going to let me forget that, are you?"

"Not in this lifetime." He grinned and rolled her over onto her back.

Caitlin paused at the threshold of her living room. It looked pleasantly lived in. She'd decorated it in muted earth tones and touches of blue.

Her gaze drifted to the stone fireplace. Beside it stood a wooden cradle. It had been lovingly hand carved and was filled with hand-stitched quilts. There was no warm little body to occupy it. But perhaps, she thought, there would be in a year or so.

She crossed the room to put a Bavarian cream pie on a table beside the camelback sofa. Then she sat down to wait for *him* to walk through the door.

She glanced out the window. Although it was only early March, spring had arrived, bringing warm days and a burst of colorful blooms. Dazzling hues painted the Southwestern sky as night approached.

It had been a good year. She loved her work with the Institute. It was all she'd hoped it would be and more. All her dreams had turned into realities.

At first, she'd worried whether Drew would be truly happy uprooting himself from New Orleans. Her concerns had been unwarranted, though. According to her husband, Houston was the *only* place to live.

Not long after they'd arrived in Houston, he'd connected with four physicians whose views on providing good, inexpensive medical care matched his own. In a way, she thought, all five of them were like throwbacks from the sixties. They'd bought and remodeled an old house in a run-down section of town that was half-commercial property and half-residential. They provided medical care on a sliding-fee scale; people paid according to what they were able to afford.

She grinned as she pictured the turn-of-the-century frame house they'd hung their shingles on. It didn't remotely resemble a medical facility. It was exactly what it looked like, a friendly, vital place where people immediately felt at ease. Patients came in droves. Drew was happily up to his earlobes in kids.

She shivered slightly. After a year of marriage, thinking of Drew still brought joy bubbling to the surface. She felt that joy rippling in ever-widening circles through her, like a pebble tossed into a quiet pool.

The sound of a finely tuned engine caught her attention. She looked out the window and saw a silver Mercedes pulling into the driveway.

She laughed softly and waited.

Drew booted the kitchen door closed. Instantly a rush of warmth, a sense of coming home, enveloped him.

Would he ever lose that feeling? he wondered. He doubted it. It was too good to grow blasé and careless about.

He set a white box on the counter. Opening it, he removed a Bavarian cream pie. Singing "Happy Anniversary to Me," he went in search of the woman who made that little song possible.

THE EDITOR'S CORNER

As winter's chilly blasts bring a rosy hue to your cheeks and remind you of the approaching holiday season, why not curl up in a cozy blanket with LOVESWEPT's own gift bag of six heartwarming romances.

The ever-popular Helen Mittermeyer leads the list with **KRYSTAL**, LOVESWEPT #516. Krystal Wynter came to Seattle to start over in a town where no one could link her with the scandalous headlines that had shattered her life. But tall, dark, and persistent Cullen Dempsey invades her privacy, claiming her with an intoxicating abandon that awakens old fears and ensnaring her in a web of desire that keeps her from running away. A moving, sensual romance—and another winner from Helen Mittermeyer!

LOVESWEPT's reputation for innovation continues as Terry Lawrence takes you right up to the stars with **EVER SINCE ADAM**, #517, set in an orbiting station in outer space! Maggie Mullins is there to observe maverick astronaut Adam Strade in the environment she helped design—not to succumb to his delicious flirting. And while Adam sweeps her off her feet in zero gravity, he fights letting her get close enough to discover his hidden pain. Don't miss this unique love story. Bravo, Terry, for a romance that's out of this world!

Please give a rousing welcome to Patricia Potter and her first LOVESWEPT, **THE GREATEST GIFT**, #518. Patricia has already garnered popular and critical success with her numerous historical romances, and in **THE GREATEST GIFT** she proves her flair with short, contemporary romance, as well. Writing about a small-town teacher isn't reporter Lane Drury's idea of a dream assignment—until she meets David Farrar. This charming rogue soon convinces her she's captured the most exciting job of all in a romance that will surely be a "keeper." Look for more wonderful stories from Patricia Potter in the year to come.

Let Joan J. Domning engulf you with a wave of passion in **STORMY'S MAN**, LOVESWEPT #519. Gayle Stromm certainly feels as if she's in over her head with Cass Starbaugh, who's six feet six inches of hard muscles, bronzed skin, and sun-streaked hair. Gayle's on vacation to escape nightmares, but caring for the injured mountain climber only makes her dream of a love she thinks she can never have. Cass can't turn down a challenge, though, and he'd do anything to prove to Stormy that she's all the woman he wants. An utterly spellbinding romance by the incomparable Joan J. Domning.

Marvelously talented Maris Soule joins our fold with the stirring **JARED'S LADY**, LOVESWEPT #520. Maris already has several romances to her credit, and you'll soon see why we're absolutely thrilled to have her. Jared North can't believe that petite Laurie Crawford is the ace tracker the police sent to find his missing niece, and, to Laurie's dismay, he insists on joining the search. She's had enough of overprotective men to last a lifetime, yet raw hunger sparks inside her at his touch. Together these two create an elemental force that will leave you breathless and looking for the next LOVESWEPT by Maris Soule.

IRRESISTIBLE, LOVESWEPT #521 by beloved author Joan Elliot Pickart, is the perfect description for Pierce Anderson. This drop-dead-gorgeous architect thinks he's hallucinating when a woman-sized chicken begs him to unzip her. But when a dream girl emerges from the feathers, he knows the fever he feels has nothing to do with the flu! Calico Smith struggles to resist the sensual power of Pierce's kissable lips. She's worked so hard for everything she has, while he's never fought for what he wanted—until now. Another fabulous romance from Joan Elliott Pickart.

And (as if these six books aren't enough) LOVESWEPT is celebrating the joyous ritual of weddings with a contest for you, a contest that will have three winners! Look for details in the January 1992 LOVESWEPTS.

Don't forget FANFARE, where you can expect three superb books this month. **THE FLAMES OF VENGEANCE** is the second book in bestselling Beverly Byrne's powerful trilogy. From rebellion plotted beneath cold, starry skies to the dark magic that stalks the sultry Caribbean night, Lila Curran's web, baited with lust and passion, is carefully being spun. Award-winning Francine Rivers delivers a compelling historical romance in **REDEEMING LOVE**. Sold into sin as a child, beautiful, tormented "Angel" never believed in love until the strong and tender Michael Hosea walked into her life. Can their radiant happiness conquer the darkest demons from her past? Much-acclaimed Sandra Brown will find a place in your heart—if she hasn't already—with **22 INDIGO PLACE**. Rebel millionaire James Paden has a dream—to claim 22 Indigo Place and its alluring owner, Laura Nolan, the rich man's daughter for whom he'd never been good enough. Three terrific books from FANFARE, where you'll find only the best in women's fiction.

As always at this season, we send you the same wishes. May your New Year be filled with all the best things in life—the company of good friends and family, peace and prosperity, and, of course, love.

Warm wishes from all of us at LOVESWEPT and FANFARE,

Nita Taublib

Nita Taublib
Associate Publisher, LOVESWEPT
Publishing Associate, FANFARE

FANFARE

FANFARE

Rosanne Bittner
_____ 28599-8 EMBERS OF THE HEART . $4.50/5.50 in Canada
_____ 29033-9 IN THE SHADOW OF THE MOUNTAINS
$5.50/6.99 in Canada
_____ 28319-7 MONTANA WOMAN .... $4.50/5.50 in Canada

Dianne Edouard and Sandra Ware
_____ 28929-2 MORTAL SINS .... $4.99/5.99 in Canada

Tami Hoag
_____ 29053-3 MAGIC .... $3.99/4.99 in Canada

Kay Hooper
_____ 29256-0 THE MATCHMAKER, ... $4.50/5.50 in Canada
_____ 28953-5 STAR-CROSSED LOVERS .. $4.50/5.50 in Canada

Virginia Lynn
_____ 29257-9 CUTTER'S WOMAN, ... $4.50/4.50 in Canada
_____ 28622-6 RIVER'S DREAM, ... $3.95/4.95 in Canada

Beverly Byrne
_____ 28815-6 A LASTING FIRE .... $4.99/ 5.99 in Canada
_____ 28468-1 THE MORGAN WOMEN .. $4.95/ 5.95 in Canada

Patricia Potter
_____ 29069-X RAINBOW .... $4.99/ 5.99 in Canada

Deborah Smith
_____ 28759-1 THE BELOVED WOMAN .. $4.50/ 5.50 in Canada
_____ 29092-4 FOLLOW THE SUN .... $4.99/ 5.99 in Canada
_____ 29107-6 MIRACLE .... $4.50/ 5.50 in Canada

Ask for these titles at your bookstore or use this page to order.

Please send me the books I have checked above. I am enclosing $ _____ (please add
$2.50 to cover postage and handling). Send check or money order, no cash or C. O. D.'s
please.

Mr./ Ms. _____

Address _____

City/ State/ Zip _____

Send order to: Bantam Books, Dept. FN, 414 East Golf Road, Des Plaines, IL 60016
Please allow four to six weeks for delivery.
Prices and availablity subject to change without notice. FN 17 - 12/91